When Linda woke up ~~and~~ realized Don Diego had been studying her.

Linda made a move to sit up, but he reached a hand to her shoulder and pressed her gently back against the seat. "Do not move. You look so relaxed, and the moonlight is on your face so that I can see you."

"When did we arrive?"

"Just a few minutes ago. You look like a little girl when you sleep."

"Have I been sleeping long?"

"About half an hour. You were smiling."

"Was I? I was dreaming about the marvelous time I had in Seville today. Thank you again. I'll remember it always."

Leaning toward her, he said softly, "Moonlight suits you. *Eres muy Linda.*"

She could see the liquid shine of his eyes. The world faded away, and she was aware only of Diego Halcón y Pizarro. Her heart skipped a beat as his hands cradled her face and his face came close. . . closer. . . .

He kissed her eyelids and cheeks, her nose and chin, and then her lips gently, sweetly. She melted against him, for he was kissing her with a tenderness that told her he cared.

FRANCES CARFI MATRANGA's short stories, articles, and poems have appeared in 300 publications, and at one time she wrote and designed greeting cards professionally. Five of her short stories and a Christian article won awards in the *Writer's Digest* annual international contests. She has won other awards, and was once a runner-up in a scriptwriting competition. Her main interest in writing is fiction.

Angel
Face

Frances Carfi Matranga

Heartsong Presents

*To my dear Aunt Sylvia Poddi and
Catherine, Esther, and Joni Kolenda
with love.*

ISBN 1-55748-501-1

ANGEL FACE

one

A strange, stunned feeling overwhelmed the young woman as she regained consciousness. She was flat on her back, and the heavenly fragrance of roses surrounded her.

She opened her eyes. *Where am I?* Carefully, she moved her head on the pillow and looked around. She was in a plain, sterile-looking room with a single window. Narrow rays of sunlight slipped through the louvers. A soft draft of air coming through a grille on the wall made the room comfortably cool.

On the bedside cabinet stood a vase of pink roses. On the other side of the bed hung a container with a tube that led to her left arm. Fear mushroomed within her. This was a hospital room! What had happened to her?

Wait now. Don't panic. In a moment I'll remember.

She waited, expecting memory to come. Nothing. Her mind was like a blank sheet of paper. Why, she couldn't remember her name!

Shocked by that realization, she sat up with a jerk. The quick movement set a hammer pounding inside her head. The room wavered. She moaned and sank back against the pillow. Lifting a hand, she gingerly felt her head and winced as her fingers touched a lump the size of a walnut on the right side. Had she been in an accident?

Cautiously, she moved first one leg, then the other.

Her body felt stiff and sore, but her bones seemed to be intact. What had happened? What hospital was this?

"Where am I?" The sound of her voice in the quiet room increased her sense of unreality. She could be in New York or California—or Timbuktu, for all she knew. She fought down the hysteria rising within her. Perhaps if she remained perfectly still it would all come back to her.

Just then the door opened and a slender, dark-haired man in a white coat entered the room. He had a pleasant face and wore gold-rimmed spectacles.

"Ah, fully awake at last," he said with a smile as he approached the bed.

He reached for her wrist and felt her pulse.

"What happened to me? Are you my doctor?"

He nodded. "Luis Perales at your service, señorita." He pulled up a chair and sat down. "You had a nasty fall. You do not remember?" He spoke with a heavy accent.

She shook her head and winced as pain shot through it.

"Easy now. No sudden movements," he cautioned. "You have a concussion. You do not recall being hit by the automobile, eh?"

"I was hit by a car?" She stared at him, incredulous. "How could I not remember a thing like that?"

"It is not unusual in concussion cases." Brown eyes regarded her kindly. "Your brain received a shock, a severe jolt, when your head hit the pavement. It is fortunate you were sideswiped by the fender rather than hit head-on. You were on the sidewalk when it happened. The vehicle mounted the curb."

"Is my concussion serious?" She could hear herself

speaking, but felt she was doing it out of habit, using words automatically.

"An x-ray examination showed no fracture of your skull, and there is no evidence of hemorrhage or pressure on the brain. We shall keep you under observation for a while to watch for complications. You have been unconscious for two days."

"Two days!"

"You were brought here Sunday. It is now Tuesday afternoon. You may have a visitor today, Diego Halcón, the man who sideswiped you. He has phoned several times to inquire about you. If you had to be in an accident," the doctor's lips quirked humorously, "better with a rich man who can afford a private room and beautiful flowers for you—eh, señorita?" It seemed odd, she thought, that both her doctor and the man responsible for her accident were Spanish. "Please, where is this hospital?"

Dr. Perales' eyes narrowed slightly. *"Sevilla,"* he said in Spanish. Then he pronounced it the English way, "Seville."

"Seville?" She repeated it, not understanding.

"You are in Andalusia, señorita. Surely you remember that?"

She stared at him incredulously. "In southern Spain? But what am I doing in Spain!" It was a cry of bewilderment. "I thought we were in the United States! I'm an American, aren't I? Oh, Doctor, I can't remember anything!" Tears trembled on her lashes.

"Please, señorita, you must not excite yourself. It is bad for your head. Yes, evidently you are an American, probably here on summer vacation." Frowning, he prompted, "You do remember your family? Friends?"

"Nothing. I remember nothing about myself! Not even my name." Her voice was shaky and tinged with hysteria. It was obvious the doctor hadn't expected total amnesia, and that in itself struck her as ominous. Perhaps her injury was more severe than the x-rays had revealed.

"My name?" she pleaded. "Surely my identification is in my handbag."

Dr. Perales shook his head. "There is no handbag, no identification. And no knowledge of any luggage at this time. It seems probable your handbag was stolen during the confusion following the accident. I see you do not wear a wedding ring. As for your name, señorita . . . ." He opened the drawer of the bedside cabinet and handed her a stainless steel ID bracelet with the inscription: *Linda*. "You were wearing this."

"Linda." She spoke the name aloud, but it brought no memories. "It could be anybody's name, for all it means to me," she said bleakly, handing back the bracelet.

"This is yours also." The doctor was holding up a stainless steel Timex wrist watch, an inexpensive model with a gray vinyl strap.

"No," she said, her chin quivering. "I don't remember having that."

Suppose she never regained her memory? A girl without a past, without identity or family and friends—the thought made her ache with loneliness, with a sad sense of loss that gathered into a lump in her throat. She swallowed painfully, struggling to control her emotions.

"I am sorry, Miss Linda," Dr. Perales said gently, replacing the items in the drawer. "I can imagine how confused you must feel. I myself—" He cut off the words, but she knew what he was thinking. The extent of her amnesia perplexed him. He hadn't expected it.

"It's as though—as though I never existed before today," she said in a half-whisper, her own words frightening her still more. "I. . .I've even forgotten what I look like."

"Oh? Well, you are in for a pleasant surprise." He smiled at her, as though glad to be able to give her one bit of good news. "You are not only young, but extremely pretty. When the color returns to your cheeks, you will be quite lovely. Your name suits you. It means 'lovely.' "

She gave him a wan smile. "Perhaps you could have the nurse bring me a mirror?"

He regarded her thoughtfully. "I think it might be wise to wait until you are stronger."

"Why? I just want to know what I look like. Oh! You think I might not recognize myself?"

That hadn't occurred to her. Bad enough not to recall her name or anything of her past life, but to look into a mirror and see only a stranger—no, she couldn't face that!

"You have had enough to upset you for the present. Your concussion is rather severe, I am afraid. But with rest and quiet, I see no reason why you should not regain your memory." Dr. Perales rose from the chair and removed Linda's IV. "One more thing." He stepped to the closet and pulled out a coral dress. The top was soiled on one side.

Linda stared at it. "Mine?"

He nodded and looked at the label. "Size 10."

Her eyes filled again.

He sighed and replaced the hanger, then came to stand beside her bed. "From your clothes, the police assumed you to be an American tourist. And here at the hospital we noticed you spoke English with an American accent."

"I was conscious when brought here? I spoke?"

"You've opened your eyes and spoken several times since the accident."

"Did I say anything that might be significant?" she asked eagerly.

"No. And you were so dazed you were not really aware of anything that went on around you. For the most part you have been unconscious until now." He glanced at his wrist watch. "I am very late in making my rounds today. I will look in on you again before I leave the hospital. Remember, no sudden movements. Good healthy sleep and quiet, that is what you need."

"And my. . .my memory will return?"

He inclined his head in response to the plea in her voice. "In time, once you have recovered from the concussion. The main thing is not to worry. Let memory return in its own good time. Now I must leave, but I will send in the nurse."

"Please ask her to bring me a glass of cold water."

When he had gone she reviewed their conversation. At least she knew her name, albeit only half a name. She spoke it softly, liking the sound of it. What kind of girl was Linda?

She held up her hands and studied them with no sense of recognition. They were slender, with smooth white skin and oval fingernails that gleamed with colorless polish. The third finger of her right hand wore what looked like a school graduation ring, probably a high school ring. She did not recognize it, and its date meant only that she had graduated some six years ago. *What did these hands do for a living?* she wondered. If her inexpensive bracelet and watch were any indication, she obviously was a working girl.

Slipping a hand beneath the covers, she explored her body under the hospital gown. Her left hip hurt dreadfully when she pressed it; the car must have sideswiped her on that side. Part of her right hip hurt also, and her right upper arm. She must have fallen on her right side. Lifting the covers, she saw black and blue marks on both sides. But contusions seemed a minor thing when compared with her loss of memory, her loss of *self.*

Sudden anger swept through her, causing her head to throb. If it were not for that man—that reckless Diego Halcón—she would be hale and hearty and able to enjoy her vacation in Spain. For his car to have climbed the curb, he must have been drunk. A rich playboy, no doubt. She would press charges.

She turned her head to look at the roses. They were lovely. But she didn't care to see Mr. Halcón just yet. It would only upset her. Seeing that her hands were clenched, she uncurled them and took a deep breath. She must remain calm and rest so her mind could heal.

A long lock of hair lay draped across one shoulder. She felt it curiously. Golden blond and wavy. Soft and silky. Her eyes were probably blue.

Please, God, let me recognize my face when I see it.

"Well, hello." A smiling nurse had entered the room, holding a glass of water. "Good to see you wide awake for a change. I'm Rosita Gonzales, the nurse in charge of you. You are in a Catholic hospital, but I am not a sister-nurse. Call me Rosita." She raised the bed and handed Linda the glass, which she drained thirstily. Rosita was a young nurse, a little on the plump side, and had bright black eyes that twinkled with good humor. Her short dark hair gave her a pert look.

"Now we'll get you cleaned up, Linda." First, the nurse brought Linda a bedpan, followed by a sponge bath, a fresh hospital gown, and a change of sheets. Rosita then raised the bed a little for comfort.

"Feel better? You've been flat on your back long enough. I know it hurts to move with all those bruises, but better black and blue than broken bones."

"I think I'd rather have a broken bone or two than this loss of memory," Linda told her.

"You mustn't worry, Linda," Rosita said firmly. "Once you've recovered from the concussion, your memory is bound to wake up."

If only I could be sure of that, Linda thought, sighing. Of course they would tell her that. Mustn't upset the patient. But the fact remained that she remembered nothing about her personal life, not even her own face. That frightened her.

A strong desire to wear her ID bracelet swept over Linda. It was the only link to her identity, and like a baby's security blanket, it might give her some small measure of comfort.

"Rosita, my bracelet in the drawer—I'd like to wear it, please."

The nurse placed it about Linda's right wrist. "Too bad it doesn't give your full name. Want to wear your watch?" She glanced at her own wristwatch. "Mine is a Timex also. I spent a year in Florida with an aunt and bought it while there. That was six years ago, and it's still running."

She wound and set Linda's watch and strapped it on her left wrist. "By the way, Señor Halcón phoned again

to ask if you were awake. I suppose the doctor told you
he's the man who knocked you down with his car. Why
don't you take a nap until he gets here. You haven't had
a normal sleep in two days." Rosita gathered up the
used linens and whisked out of the room. Soon an
orderly appeared and wheeled away the intravenous
equipment.

Linda looked at her ID bracelet. *I'm Linda.* Half a
name was better than none.

She fingered her wristwatch, lower lip caught between
her teeth. How could a young working girl afford a trip
to Europe? And why Spain? Why not France or Swit-
zerland or the Holy Land? Did Spain hold some special
significance for her?

*How strange! I can't recall my parents and friends or
my home, yet I know the names of countries, the days in
the week, and the months in the year. I haven't forgotten
how to read time or the printed word. And I still know
God. Please help me through this ordeal, dear Lord.*

How long would it take to recuperate fully? Days?
Weeks? Months? The thought of existing in a vacuum
for months brought a faint cry of protest to her lips.
How would she live in the meantime?

Señor Halcón, what have you done to me!

Her head was beginning to throb, reminding Linda
that she mustn't get upset. The nurse was right. She felt
weak and needed sleep. Her eyelids drooped. Wouldn't
it be marvelous to go to sleep and awaken refreshed
and in full possession of her memory?

When she opened her eyes, a stranger was sitting
beside her bed. Seeing she was awake, he went to open
the louvers halfway, letting sunlight spill into the room.
Back at her bedside, she heard him murmur, "Spanish

eyes."

At once the song "Blue Spanish Eyes" came to her mind. Was that what he meant? But, of course, she wasn't Spanish.

He was tall and wore an expertly tailored blue and gray plaid jacket with azure silk tie and blue trousers. Dark of hair and complexion, with lustrous midnight eyes, high cheekbones, and a forceful jaw, he carried an unmistakable air of authority. Trying not to be over-awed by him, Linda returned his gaze, noticing a touch of the orient in the way his eyes were shaped. Quite magnificent eyes they were.

"I am Diego Halcón y Pizarro," he introduced himself.

"How do you do?" she said. "Thank you for the roses."

"I would have come sooner, but you would not have been able to speak to me," he said, sitting down.

"About the accident, how did it happen? I don't remember."

"I regret it very much, señorita. It is most unfortunate that you were on the sidewalk at the very moment I swerved my car." His accented baritone voice was pleasant to Linda's ears. "I was trying to avoid hitting a child who had darted into the street. I did not see you until too late."

So he had not been drinking. Somehow she felt relieved that the accident had not been due to negligence. He did not seem the sort of man who would permit himself to lose control of his faculties.

"I am thankful you have no broken bones," he continued. "Dr. Perales told me over the telephone that you might not recall what happened. He is a friend of mine. I asked him to look after you. He says patients with concussion often cannot remember what happened to them. Do not let that disturb you."

"I wish it were that simple."

"What do you mean?"

"It isn't only the accident I can't recall." Linda held up her wrist. "I wouldn't know my name if it weren't for this ID bracelet. But it doesn't give my family name. Just Linda."

"Are you saying you do not know who you are?"

"I'm afraid so. I can't remember my parents or friends or where I live." She could feel her throat tightening as tears threatened again. "My past life is a complete blank . . .even what I look like."

"You do not remember your own face? But this is incredible!" The man's black brows arched toward his hairline in astonishment, and for a moment he seemed at a loss for words.

"There must have been identification in my handbag," she said. "But it seems to have disappeared. The handbag, I mean."

He shook his head slowly from side to side, incredulity still stamped upon his features. "We searched for it at the site of the accident, but none was found. Perhaps you were not carrying one."

"I doubt that. It seems unlikely a woman would go out without her handbag."

"Well, then, it may have been picked up by some passing gypsy taking advantage of all the excitement." The dark eyes studied her face. "You are quite certain you remember nothing? Nothing at all?"

"Not about my personal life." Did he doubt her word?

He stroked his chin, contemplating her through narrowed eyes. "This total blankness you speak of, Luis is aware of it by now?"

"The doctor? Yes, I told him."

"And what did he say?"

"That I'll recover my memory in time." Her lips quivered. "I hope so. It would be awful to spend the rest of my life like this." She turned her face away, biting her lip.

A blanket of silence fell over them. She heard the scrape of her visitor's chair and footsteps crossing the tiled floor. Turning her head on the pillow, she saw he was standing at the window, looking out. She could sense tension emanating from him; it showed in his bearing, his clenched hands. He seemed—angry?

Just then Dr. Perales appeared in the doorway.

"Ah, Don Diego, I am glad I caught you. You have spoken with the patient? Excuse us, señorita."

They began conversing in low tones by the window, and at first Linda could not hear what they were saying. Then their voices began to rise.

"But why is her entire memory blanked out?" Don Diego was demanding. "You told me there was no pressure on the brain and no hemorrhaging."

"Listen, my friend, amnesia affects people in different ways. At least Linda is rational. I once heard about a car accident that caused a mature woman to have complete amnesia. She woke up like a baby. She knew nothing, did not recognize family, did not know what 'husband' or 'son' meant. She was completely childlike with an entirely different personality. Doctors did not know if or when she would remember the past. I hope she has by now. As for Linda, I believe she will recover."

By this time, it had dawned on Linda that she was listening to a conversation in Spanish. And she had understood every word!

"What I am getting at, Luis, is this: could this girl be putting on an act?"

"You mean pretending she has amnesia?"

"Either that or exaggerating its severity."

Linda gasped inwardly. *How dare that man say such a thing!*

"I do not think she is pretending, Diego. Remember, she has been unconscious the better part of two days. And why should she exaggerate her condition?"

"Is it not obvious? She probably has hopes of suing me for all she can get. The more severe the amnesia and the longer it lasts, the stronger her case."

"She does not strike me as that kind of person. Such a sweet face—"

"Ah, I see you have not yet learned that women are masters in the art of subterfuge. And the ones who look like angels, they especially bear watching. Now tell me, does your patient know I am wealthy?"

"I did refer to it jokingly by pointing out that only a rich man would arrange for her to have a private room and flowers."

"I see. Now think carefully before you answer this next question. Did she claim amnesia before or after she learned I am wealthy?"

A pause. "After. But I wish you would not jump to conclusions. What do you intend to do? And where does the girl go from here? Alone in a foreign country and penniless—what if her mind is still impaired when I discharge her from the hospital?"

"She will come to my home, of course. Since I am responsible for her injuries, I will see to it that she is provided for until she is completely well. You feel she will regain her memory, eh?"

"Although I cannot guarantee it, I feel optimistic about her case. I discussed it with a colleague, and he agrees that when the concussion heals, memory should return, although perhaps not all at once."

"Good. As you know, I am spending the week in town. I would like to return home on Saturday and take the girl with me."

"I will let you know on Friday after I give her a psychological test and physical examination."

"Very well. And I intend to keep a sharp eye on her. Between Josefa and myself, we will soon know if she is misrepresenting this mental condition of hers. No woman is going to make a fool of me."

Burning with anger and humiliation, Linda had to bite her tongue to control it. Arrogant know-it-all!

"You are condemning the girl in advance," Dr. Perales reproached the Don. "She is my patient, and I do not want you upsetting her."

"I intend giving her the benefit of the doubt until she makes a slip that proves otherwise. Meanwhile, do all you can for her."

They turned toward Linda.

"Please forgive our speaking in Spanish, Miss Linda," the doctor said. "When two Spaniards get together, the native tongue comes automatically. Are you feeling rested?"

"Yes, thank you," she said, trying to keep her voice steady. "I slept a little before Mr. Halcón arrived."

He nodded. "Get as much sleep as possible. I will see you in the morning. Coming, Diego?"

"*Sí.* Adiós, señorita."

Left alone, Linda replayed the discussion she had

overheard between the two Spanish *caballeros*, wondering how she had learned their language so well. And did she really have the look of an angel, albeit with an empty head? The whimsical thought made her smile. Now that she believed Dr. Perales was sincerely optimistic about the return of her memory, her hopes soared.

Linda thought again about Don Diego's low opinion of women. Poor Josefa. No doubt he kept her under his thumb. And he intended that both he and his wife would keep a sharp eye on this American girl, did he? What was it going to be like, living under the roof of a man who suspected her of being a liar and a fraud?

two

A beaming Rosita came hurrying into Linda's room. "Good news! A Mrs. Torre just phoned. She rented a room last Saturday to a blond American named Linda Monroe. When there was no sign of the girl for two days, she called here to see if anyone answering your description had been admitted. She was shocked to hear you'd lost your memory. Anyway, your things are at her house."

"Thank goodness! I'll have some clothes to wear." Linda's smile widened. "Monroe? Hmm, I like it. Linda Monroe. What a relief to know my name! Did she say anything else about me?"

"You told her you're from New York and that your parents are dead. And your room is paid up for the week. She wanted to know if you're going back there. Dr. Perales told her no, and asked her to have your things dropped off here at the hospital. It seems you're on vacation for three weeks, but Mrs. Torre said you were vague about where you'd be staying all that time. You didn't come with a tour group. That's all she could tell us about you."

"Three weeks? That's a long vacation. Does Señor Halcón know all this?"

"Not yet. He left just before the call came in. What an attractive man! I hear he owns a plantation in the valley south of here. You may be convalescing there." She leaned over to take a deep whiff of the roses. "Mmm, gorgeous. One might as well get sideswiped by a rich man as a poor one."

"Seems I've heard that before," said Linda.

"Yeah? Let me add he might as well be handsome as not."

"What difference does that make?"

"In case he turns out to be your Prince Charming. I'm a sentimental romanticist at heart," the saucy nurse admitted with a grin. "Once I got a look at that *hombre,* I couldn't help fantasizing about you two. Heroine accidently struck down by prince. Loses memory. He looks after her. They fall in love, marry, and live happily ever after. What a striking pair, you so fair and he dark! And he does have the lordly air of a prince, I noticed."

Linda couldn't resist her cheery nurse, even though she was spouting nonsense. "From something he said, I gather he's already married."

"Aw, too bad." Rosita made a clown face of disappointment.

"Do you have a prince?" Linda asked her.

"I'm leaving here next week to take charge of his office." The young woman rolled her expressive eyes and whispered, "It's Luis Perales."

"Really? I like him."

"He's got heart, that doctor. Linda, I've been thinking. I believe there are some things the subconscious never forgets. If you have a special talent, you still have it, even though you don't remember. You will discover it all over again. And if you're a person of good character, you still are. Have you remembered anything at all?"

"Some sad generalities," Linda told her. "Famines, earthquakes, riots, the lack of morals nowadays.

Impersonal things, but without any point of view. They seem the memory of someone else, somehow acquired by me."

"Pretty soon the personal memories and feelings will return. You'll see," Rosita encouraged. "Meanwhile I'll be praying for you."

Two suitcases were delivered for Linda. Rosita had them brought to her room. One was medium size, of blue vinyl and plaid zippered cloth; the other was small, its brown vinyl scuffed and worn.

"It's like I've never seen them before," Linda said. "Just lift out a few items from one of them, will you, Rosita? If I don't recognize them, I probably won't recognize anything. But, please, do look for my passport. I hope I wasn't carrying it in my lost handbag."

They both sighed with relief when Rosita found the passport in one of the shirred pockets of the larger bag. Opening it, Linda read her name aloud. Her address in White Plains, New York, meant nothing to her. Beneath that, where it said to give the name and address of someone to notify in case of death or accident, she had left the spaces blank.

"It looks like I have no family at all," she said in a small voice. Slowly, she turned the page to her birth date. She was twenty-four, born in April, although the girl in the passport photo looked more like eighteen. The eyes were brown, not blue.

She stared at the picture for a long time, hoping the cloud over her mind would lift. Then, swallowing, she said to her new friend, "You can't imagine how it feels to know you're looking at a photograph of your own face and not recognize it. I've got to remember me, make myself real." Tears shone in her eyes.

"You're plenty real," said Rosita, "and you *will* remember. Look, here's your return airline ticket. *¡Qué mala suerte!* Rotten luck to end up in the hospital the day after arrival." She held up a blouse and skirt, a robe and slippers, and a few other items. Nothing seemed familiar to Linda.

"Well, at least you can wear one of your own nightgowns. I'll leave out your robe and slippers. Ah, here's a hand mirror. Want to look at the pretty lady?"

Linda hesitated. Then she shrugged. "I might as well, now that I've seen the photograph."

Her hand trembled a little as she lifted the mirror. The eyes looking back at her were startlingly dark against the pallor of her face. No wonder the Don had called them Spanish eyes. Her face was oval, the nose straight and slender, the mouth small with full lips. How young and vulnerable she looked, this stranger!

She now knew her name and what she looked like, yet no chord of memory echoed in her mind. Once her concussion healed, she'd be fine, she told herself, and all this would seem like a bad dream. She had to believe that.

"See, you're a doll," Rosita proclaimed, placing the mirror in the drawer of the cabinet. "You rest now. I'm going home." She winked. "You can be sure you're a special case or they wouldn't let me spend so much time with you. Señor Halcón must have influence around here."

Linda dismissed him with a shrug. "Good night, Rosita."

When Dr. Perales stopped by in the morning, he seemed

pleased with Linda's appearance. "Your eyes look brighter today. You are feeling better, yes? Your belongings have turned up and now you know a little more about yourself. Things are looking up, señorita. Let us hope you can go home on Saturday. Then I will want to see you again for a final checkup."

"Home?" She knew full well what he meant.

"Don Diego's home in the country. You need a place to stay for a while, and you will not be the only woman there." Seeing reluctance in her expression, the doctor continued his urgings. "The fresh country air and quiet life will be good for you and bring back the roses in your cheeks. I could not recommend a more suitable environment for convalescing. With servants to attend to you, you need only rest and get well."

Linda cleared her throat. "Do you think he would arrange for me to stay in Seville?"

"Alone? I doubt it. Diego wishes to watch over you, Miss Linda. To make certain no complications arise, you understand."

I understand only too well, Linda thought. Aloud she said, "If I went back to Mrs. Torre's house, I wouldn't be alone."

"I cannot agree to that. I am sorry, señorita, but either you convalesce at the Don's home or else spend extra time in hospital. Either way I will know you are in good hands." The doctor spoke so firmly that Linda knew there was no use trying to persuade him.

"Besides, Diego would not hear of it," he added. "He feels responsible for you. You should be grateful. Is there something about him that disturbs you?"

"I. . .I don't think he likes me."

"Oh? Why?"

"It's. . .an impression I have."

"He thinks you are very pretty."

Linda lowered her gaze, wishing she hadn't brought up the subject.

The doctor dropped it tactfully. He felt the lump on her head.

"It is going down." Looking into her eyes, he said, "You have to admit it is to your advantage that Don Diego is a man of means. Suppose a poor man without insurance had caused the accident. As it is, you need not concern yourself about money or medical expenses. And when you are well, Diego will arrange a fair settlement for you. He is a man of integrity."

The day passed slowly for Linda.

Wednesday also.

On Thursday, she was able to get out of bed to use the bathroom and stretch her legs. It felt good to get out of her room and take a walk down the hall with her nurse. On the way back, she felt a bit wobbly and held on to Rosita's arm.

"I'm beginning to feel like a mother hen with her chick," Rosita remarked as she helped Linda into bed. "You're on my mind even when I'm away from the hospital. It bothers me that you're so alone. What you need, Linda, is a good man in your life. I hope it's Señor Halcón."

Linda made a face at her. "Didn't I tell you—"

"Don't you think he's a fine-looking gentleman?" Rosita interrupted, placing a hand over her heart and pretending to swoon. "Did you notice what wonderful eyes he has? And rich besides. What more could any girl want?"

"How about love?" Linda suggested, smiling at the girl's theatrics.

"Who couldn't fall in love with a man like that? Do you realize how exciting your case is? Like something in the movies. Even the sisters are whispering about it."

"Seriously now, how can you ignore the fact that the man is married," Linda scolded. "Don't the nuns know that?"

"Surprise! He's not!" Rosita's eyes expressed delight. Linda caught her breath.

"The prince needs a wife, see?" Rosita went on. "I asked Dr. Perales. He told me the Don lives with his sister. He's a bachelor, and she's never married. So there!" She left the room giggling.

That afternoon, Linda had a visitor, a lanky young man who couldn't have been more than eighteen. He greeted her in Spanish and expressed regrets over her misfortune. She did not know him, though he obviously knew her.

"Ah, Linda, I see you do not remember me," he said ruefully. "I am Sancho Torre. You took a room at our house last Saturday and spoke to me and my mother in Spanish. My English is poor." He sat close to her.

"It's nice of you to visit me." Linda glanced toward the door as she spoke in his language, hoping Rosita wouldn't show up. "I'm sorry I don't remember you."

"You agreed to let me show you around Seville," he told her, "but then you were hurt the next morning. Won't you come back to my house when you are discharged from here?"

"Dr. Perales wants me to convalesce at the home of Señor Halcón, the man responsible for my condition.

I'm being discharged on Saturday, I believe."

"But, Linda, I must see you again!" The youth leaned toward her, his thin face intense. "Don't you know I love you?"

"What? After knowing me for just a few hours? Don't be ridiculous."

He made an impatient gesture. "What does time matter? Almost from the moment we met I knew you were special. Please, you must not laugh at me."

His big brown eyes were solemn, and she sobered at once. He was young, after all, and teenagers felt things keenly.

"I'm sorry, Sancho. I'm in Spain only temporarily. And I'm older than you."

"You do not look it. And what does age matter when two people find each other?" His hand closed over hers. "You remember nothing?" He searched her face, leaned forward and said softly, "You do not recall the joy we found together in our kisses, in the warmth of our embraces?"

Linda gasped and jerked her hand from his, shocked almost speechless.

"You do not remember. But why should it upset you?" Sancho straightened up in the chair, looking puzzled. "You are an American, and in your country couples are free to show affection for each other. But with you and me it was something special, Linda. Listen—"

"I don't want to hear!" she cut in hoarsely. "Please go now." She turned her face away from him; it felt on fire, and her head was beginning to hurt.

All was still for a long moment. His chair scraped the floor as he stood up. "I will see you again, Linda." She heard his footsteps leave the room.

What kind of girl am I that I would throw myself into a stranger's arms mere hours after I'd met him? I can't believe it; he must be lying.

But why would he lie to her?

Suddenly Linda felt glad she was leaving Seville—if she passed the next day's physical and psychological tests.

Please, Lord, help me. I've got to pass those tests.
She did.

Don Diego had arranged to pick up Linda after breakfast on Saturday. She wore a crushproof, two-piece dress made of polyester that looked like silk. Patterned in green and gold on a chocolate background, it emphasized the color of her hair. Rosita gently brushed the silky, side-parted hair she had shampooed the day before. The natural waves cascaded several inches below Linda's shoulders.

"Such lovely hair. I'm going to miss you, Linda. I'll look forward to seeing you when you come to the doctor's office for your next checkup."

"You've been very kind, Rosita. I'll always remember you."

An orderly came for Linda's luggage and to tell them Señor Halcón was in the waiting room. They went along the corridor to the elevator. Linda's heart thudded. The Don had no idea she was aware of his negative feelings toward her.

Don Diego greeted the girls and waited while Linda hugged her nurse and doctor and said goodbye to several nuns who had gathered at the desk to see her off. The Don wheeled Linda outside to a tan station wagon. He helped her into the beige-upholstered front seat, tipped the orderly, and put away the luggage. Then he slid in beside Linda.

As the Don switched on the ignition and put the car in gear, Linda noticed someone on a parked motorcycle watching them. It was Sancho.

Their eyes met.

Linda quickly looked away and did not relax until the car pulled out of the hospital grounds and the motorcycle turned in the opposite direction.

"I have been informed of what you have learned about yourself," Don Diego said. "You still have two weeks before your flight home. Perhaps your memory will return by then, eh?" The look he turned on her was quizzical. "Why did you tell the doctor you wished to remain in Seville?"

The question took Linda by surprise. What could she say without lying?

"Well. . .it would be less trouble for you, wouldn't it?"

"It is no trouble, señorita. There is no reason why you should not come home with me." He spoke with the authority of one whose decisions were never questioned. "How else can I be sure of your welfare? It was my vehicle that injured you, and since you have no family and are alone in Spain, it is my duty to look after you. Furthermore, you were discharged into my care, and I have already paid the medical bills so far. You understand?"

"Yes." Linda's tone was meek now that she'd had a change of heart about remaining in the city. Going to the Don's country estate would put many miles between her and that intense boy on the motorcycle. But to live under this man's roof knowing how he felt about her was going to be uncomfortable.

The Spanish morning was gold-washed, with the sky a gentian blue. The car was pleasantly air-conditioned. Watching out the window, Linda viewed narrow twisting streets and green foliage cascading everywhere on stucco walls. She saw orange trees shading the splashing fountains of a plaza, and through wrought-iron grilles she caught glimpses of patios vivid with flowers.

"Seville looks like a lovely old city. It's the capital of Andalusia, isn't it? I wish I could tour it."

"Since I am bringing you back for a checkup a week from Monday, I could show you some of the highlights of the city then, if you like," Don Diego offered unexpectedly.

"Why, thank you. I'd like that very much. I can't help wondering what brought me to Seville. I shouldn't think a tourist would come to the hottest part of Spain in July."

"Andalusia is the heart of the mystery of Spain, señorita, and Seville is the closest you can get to that heart. It is the real Spain, and the young and healthy are willing to brave the heat to spend time in this delightful city. You must not leave our country without sightseeing in Seville. I would like you to see the charming former Jewish district called Santa Cruz, where Murillo, the artist, once lived. And the *Calle de las Sierpes*, Seville's most interesting street. Everybody snacks there, since dinner is served late in Spain."

"How late?"

"Ten o'clock or so, except in hospital. But at my home, we dine at nine."

"Even that seems awfully late to me. When do you eat lunch?"

"Around two."

"Tell me more about Andalusia," Linda prompted.

"It is yet untamed, with gypsies still living in caves in the hills. Spanish women in the more modern northern cities wander about on their own, but here in the south we revere the old traditions and are more careful of our women. In few countries does history live so vividly. Our roots are not fully broken away from the ways of the Moors. They ruled here for almost eight hundred years, and it shows in many ways—in our music, our homes, and in our attitudes toward women."

The Don's eyes gleamed as he flashed a glance at Linda. "The women in America are aggressive, no longer needle-and-thread homemakers. Here in Andalusia, women remain content to be the heart and soul of the home. They take pride in this, for it is the wife and mother who makes a house a home."

"Yet you have no wife, señor?" Linda dared ask. At once she felt him go taut and saw his lips compress.

With a short laugh and a lightness she felt was forced, he said, "Some men marry young and some not so young. I am thirty-five, but there is yet time."

"You are very particular, I take it," she murmured.

"Very."

She dared not pursue the subject and turned to the window. They were driving in the country, and the land sulked beneath the hot kiss of the sun. They passed small villages and soon the scenery became more pastoral. Linda saw a shepherd with his flock on a hillside, and goats whose neck bells clanged with every leap.

Soon they were entering a fertile region where men and women in wide-brimmed straw hats worked in ter-raced fields. As the station wagon passed donkeys bur-

dened with wood or vegetables, Linda saw close-up the
weather-browned faces of the Andalusians. The men
wore country smocks and broad-brimmed felts. They
saluted as the car went by.

A little later, Don Diego informed Linda they were
entering his estate. The land was richly planted with
barley, rye, oats, maize, clover, and olive trees. Linda
saw many groves of the gnarled trees. In the midst of it
all was a community with lime-washed houses and a
village square where several women were filling their
water jugs at the public pump. People passed back and
forth across the square and children played there.

"How picturesque," Linda exclaimed. "What is the
name of this village?"

"Aldea de Halcón." Don Diego was driving slowly
through the main road. "My family built this village.
Most of the inhabitants work for me, as did their ancestors for my ancestors."

So even a community bore the name of this autocratic
Spaniard. He was the *patrono* here, and these people
depended upon him for their livelihood.

Linda saw a church, a tiny post office, and some small
stores and cafés. The sun sparkled on the whitewashed
walls of the quaint houses, and geraniums and vines
tumbled from window grilles. Several dark-clad elderly women sat in doorways sewing or embroidering,
appearing to Linda like figures out of the distant past.

The Don increased their speed as they continued along
the valley road. Olive trees were everywhere, and sheep
and cattle grazed on slopes. *There must be thousands
of acres of Halcón territory,* thought Linda.

"You cultivate mainly olives, I see. Do you make olive
oil?" she asked.

The Don nodded. "We have our own processing plant and warehouse. We value the olive tree highly. Spain supplies one-third of the world's olive oil."

Linda leaned back in her seat and closed her eyes. Trying to see everything out the window had been a strain on her.

"You are feeling weak, señorita?"

"I feel like a piece of tired elastic," she murmured. "It's the first time I've sat up for two hours at a stretch."

He smiled at her whimsy. "Soon we will turn on the path that leads to my house. By the way, did seeing your suitcases and their contents bring back some remembrance?"

"None," she said, looking directly at him.

"When the concussion heals, eh?"

She perceived a note of sarcasm in his tone. "I hope so," she said, nervously clasping her hands together on her lap. What if the dark net over her mind refused to lift? Would he believe it? Or would he come right out and accuse her of being a fraud?

three

Ahead, flanking an archway, loomed high whitewashed walls shawled with eye-catching scarlet blossoms. Wrought-iron gates stood open, and the station wagon moved in under the archway into the huge enclosed patio centered by a marble fountain. Two sculptured boys, one on each side, held basins to catch water that overflowed into the large main basin. Shading the fountain and the benches surrounding it was a tall tree, its branches laden with yellow bell-flowers.

Linda saw palm, fig, and orange trees, golden allamanda, and white oleanders edged with burgundy. She caught a flash of colorful wings and heard the singing of birds.

A noble mansion of several stories enclosed the tiled patio on three sides. Each story had its own outside gallery, reached by a black wrought-iron staircase. The railings and windows were ornately grilled, the iron fashioned into arabesque patterns. Fronting the ground floor above three shallow steps was a veranda behind an arcade of Moorish arches and columns. Outdoor furniture was arranged in its inviting shade. The air was laden with the scents of many flowers, and Linda caught her breath in wonder at the beauty surrounding her.

The Don went around to her side of the car to assist her. "Welcome to *La Casa de Halcón*," he said. "I was born in this house. It is Moorish and centuries old, but it has been kept in good repair. We have modernized it with conveniences, but it still retains its oriental charm. Would it surprise you, señorita, to learn that my family traces its ancestry back to the days of the Moors? In those days the courts in Spain rivaled those in Baghdad."

Yes, thought Linda, *one could see a touch of the Arab in the shape of the eyes, the dark skin. It was not difficult to imagine him in the flowing robes of the desert or with a turban on that proud dark head.*

"It's beautiful here." Suddenly everything wavered in front of Linda's eyes, and she clutched at his arm. His hand shot out and gripped her other arm to steady her.

"You feel ill?"

She closed her eyes. "Dizzy."

"Shall I carry you?"

"Oh, no! It was just for a moment." She let go of him, alarmed at the thought of being held in his arms.

The hand holding her arm dropped to his side. "You must rest as soon as you have met my sister."

He gathered her suitcases and ushered her into the house. Setting down the luggage in the cool, arcaded hall, he motioned Linda toward a high-backed chair of heavy dark wood upholstered in Spanish leather that had been dyed burgundy.

"Sit down, Señorita Monroe, while I get Josefa. She will know which room to give you."

While he was gone, Linda glanced about. Her attention was arrested by a large, ancient tapestry hanging on the wall opposite her. The woven scene depicted an olive tree with a fierce hawk and a gentle white dove resting on one of its branches. The dove nestled against the bird of prey as though for protection.

How incongruous, she thought.

Her admiring glance touched upon an ornately framed mirror, carved tables, cabinets, and chairs that shone from continual polishing with the beeswax she could smell. The floor was covered with arabesque tiles that gleamed with color in contrast to the white walls. From great earthenware pots grew crimson azaleas that made vivid splashes of color against the arcade columns. At the far end, a wide stairway swept up to a three-sided gallery that overlooked the hall. The center wall of the gallery was hung with portraits and was flanked by Moorish archways that led into other wings of the house.

As Linda looked about with wide eyes, she could sense the past clinging to the mansion and could almost hear footsteps whispering through the corridors of time. No doubt these walls held captive some of the traditions of bygone days.

Doors opened from each side of the entrance hall, and through one of these came Don Diego and a gaunt woman who walked with a limp, followed by a man-servant. Clad entirely in black, the Don's sister appeared to be a few years older than he, an austere-looking individual with penetrating black eyes and hair equally dark.

As her chilly eyes examined Linda, the woman's plain features spasmed in alarm. She quickly assumed a poker face, but Linda knew she had not been mistaken. With sinking heart, she wondered why the mere sight of her was so disturbing to the Don's sister.

Introduced by her brother as Doña Josefa, she spoke to Linda in precise, accented English, "We trust you will recover quickly, Miss Monroe. If you will come with me, I will show you to your room so you can rest. You will hear the gong announcing lunch." She pointed to the bronze instrument beside the stairway.

"The young lady had a dizzy spell when we arrived.

It might be well for her to have lunch in her room today," Don Diego suggested. "You look weary, señorita. You must not overdo your first day out of hospital."

Linda nodded gratefully. She felt drained, eager to get out of her clothes and lie down.

Doña Josefa led the way up the stairs with a rustle of bombazine. She seemed to Linda a figure out of the Victorian age, the sort of stiff, precise character one seldom ran into in this modern day.

The manservant trailed behind them, carrying the luggage. They turned into the left corridor and proceeded toward the rear.

"My brother and I have rooms in the right wing. I will give you an outer room on this side with a private balcony, where you might enjoy taking breakfast. Do you wish coffee or hot chocolate in the mornings?"

"Coffee, please."

Doña Josefa pointed to a door at the end of the corridor. "That leads to the rear gallery overlooking the outbuildings." She opened a door to her left and ushered Linda into a cool, dim room. The servant set down the suitcases near the bed and retreated. Doña Josefa limped to a tall window and parted the draperies to let in the light.

"You will find the bathroom directly across the hall," she said. "The supply of water varies with the amount required for watering the plantation. Water is precious in this region and is pumped down at considerable expense from the mountains. You will have to take it as it comes. Should you need anything, use the bell-pull beside the bed. You can summon your breakfast with it in the morning. If the room becomes too warm, the switch to the ceiling fan is near the door. A maid will bring up your lunch by two o'clock. Any questions, Miss

Monroe?"

"Are there other members of the family for me to meet?"

"There is only Juanito, a nephew. He is twelve. His father was the younger of my two brothers. He perished several years ago in an air disaster, with his wife and two small daughters. It was only by the grace of God that Juanito's life was spared."

"I'm so sorry. And your parents, are they living?"

Doña Josefa hesitated. She said briefly, "They lost their lives some half dozen years ago. Another tragedy. You will please not bring up the subject of our parents to my brother, as he is very sensitive about it. Time has not dulled the pain for him."

He must have loved his parents very much, thought Linda. Evidently this family had suffered much heartache.

Doña Josefa searched her face. "You remember nothing of your past?"

"Nothing." Linda could sense the skepticism behind the question. She wondered if Don Diego had already passed on his reservations about her to his sister.

Linda sighed in relief when the bedroom door closed behind the black-clad figure. Hostility hid underneath that courteous manner, stronger even than Don Diego's subtle antagonism.

She glanced about the spacious room. Several scatter rugs lay on the tiled floor. The massive old furniture of Spanish oak looked as though it would last another century. Everything was immaculate. The Doña evidently kept a close eye on the work of the servants, demanding nothing short of perfection.

The double bed had a canopy that matched the apple-green brocaded spread, and yards of netting hung from the carved posts. The windows were draped in apple-green brocade, and from the high ceiling hung lamps that had an oriental look about them—the Moorish influence again.

Linda stepped out through French doors to the balcony. Black wrought-iron formed a lace-like cage around the balcony, and within its enclosure stood a pair of cane chairs and a circular table. Growing out of a large earthenware pot and twining itself in and out of the ornamental iron was a honeysuckle vine that spiced the air with its sweet perfume. A towering camphor tree provided shade over the table.

How charming, thought Linda. *A lovely place to have breakfast or dally with a book.* She could see the glint of water courses used for irrigation and a vegetable garden. Beyond were the ubiquitous olive trees. In the distance rose the cool, jagged sierras.

Linda went out to the corridor to the rear gallery. It ran the width of the house, and from there she had a clear view of the barn, stable, sheds, warehouses, and other outbuildings. Men and boys were bustling about, and she could hear the sounds of farm animals. A large, wolfish-looking dog lay in the shade of a palm tree, and birds nested in the jutting eaves of the buildings. Pigeons and chickens strutted about the grounds.

Returning indoors, Linda fingered the toiletries of brass and crystal on her dressing table. She leaned forward to study the face that looked back at her from the shield-shaped mirror. Again she felt that peculiar sense of detachment. It was like confronting a stranger or mere acquaintance.

How dark her eyes against her fair complexion! Her hair was golden, but her eyebrows and lashes were brown. Was her hair dyed? Her face held a disarming look of innocence that gave her that angelic appearance the Don had mentioned. Linda smiled at her reflection, pleased with her looks.

She took off her dress and zipped into her floral robe. She turned back the bed covers and lay down. How good the mattress felt beneath her weary body!

A sound straight out of the *Arabian Nights* awakened Linda. As the gong called a second time and she lay listening to its exotic echo, she had the peculiar sensation of having left the modern world and wandered into another era.

The fancy made her smile. She glanced at her wristwatch. Almost two o'clock. Famished, she lay back to await lunch. Soon there came a tap on the door and a young maid entered bearing a legged tray. Linda sat up and banked the pillows behind her back.

"*Buenos dias,* señorita. Me Pepa." The girl smiled at her shyly and set the tray before her. Seeing the luggage, she said, "After *siesta*, me put away," indicating the wardrobe.

"Thank you, Pepa." Linda pointed to the ceiling fan. "Please turn it on as you leave."

The girl nodded, curtsied, and withdrew.

After saying grace, Linda studied the courses on her tray: *gazpacho,* a cold soup specialty of Andalusia made with diced vegetables and croutons; *paella,* a tasty saffron rice dish with assorted shellfish; and crisp-fried *calamares* or squid.

So, she was familiar with Spanish cuisine as well as the language. Was she part Spanish?

Don Diego had remarked on her Spanish eyes when he first looked into them, as if he recognized them instantly. How odd!

She dug into her food with gusto, finishing off with

fruit punch and an apple tart. It was the most she had eaten all week. Putting aside the tray, Linda lay back, feeling content. She might as well enjoy the luxuries of her visit, for once the dark curtain lifted from her mind, this would end.

If only Don Diego were not harboring suspicions about her, she reflected wistfully. Being alone and handicapped in a strange country, it would be comforting to be able to think of him as a friend.

Linda woke up after three, surprised that she had dozed off again. Rising, she straightened the bed, then put on a blue T-shirt and a pair of jeans and ran a comb through her hair. She switched off the ceiling fan and made her exit from the corridor to the rear gallery. Stairs led down from both ends of the gallery, and she descended to stretch her legs a bit.

It was still siesta and all was quiet beneath the sultry heat of the sun. Even the dog had fallen asleep beneath the palm tree. The need for a siesta break was obvious. Without it, Linda realized, it would be difficult for the workers to get through the day. She decided this was not the time to explore the outbuildings, in case there were men who brought their lunch and took their rest on the premises.

She walked around the side of the house, past a patio, and went through the front gates into the courtyard. It was lovely behind the high walls covered with bright flower-shawls, the kind of walls erected by the Moors to keep out intruders and to seclude their women.

It was cooler in the courtyard, too, for there were trees and shrubs to provide shade. Even the fountain helped lower the temperature. Still, the heat was more than Linda was accustomed to, and she could feel tiny beads of moisture forming on her brow.

She strolled about fingering scented myrtle, scarlet hibiscus, and other blossoms she could not name. Never had she seen such huge blossoms, such brilliant colors, and the delight she felt was almost intoxicating. The courtyard garden seemed to her a bit of Spanish heaven.

"Lovely," she murmured, leaning forward to sniff at a shrub covered with tiny, sweet-smelling flowers.

"You seem to be enjoying our garden, señorita."

Linda caught her breath and turned to find the Don standing only a few feet away. She wished he wouldn't walk so silently, like a jungle cat tracking its prey.

His shirt was partly unbuttoned, and she could see the fine mesh of dark hair that rose toward the brown column of his throat. His gaze swept over her jeans and came to rest upon her face.

"You look refreshed," he said. "I take it you slept?"

She nodded.

"And did you eat well?"

"I sure did."

"Ah, so you enjoy Spanish cuisine."

"Very much."

"Let us sit down."

They selected a bench shaded by the tree of golden bell-flowers.

"Do you wear those pants often?" Don Diego asked Linda.

"Why. . .I suppose so, since they're part of my wardrobe. I'm comfortable in these. Do you disapprove of jeans on women?"

"In my opinion, it detracts from a woman's femininity."

Linda was silent for a moment, attempting to evaluate the matter from the point of view of a conservative Spanish man.

She said, "Since you disapprove of my jeans, Don Diego, I'll not wear them again while a guest in your home. Unless necessary for some reason."

He looked at her with eyebrows raised. "Is this a liberated *norte americana* speaking?"

"Too much liberty can lead to bad manners, I'm afraid, and to displease one's host deliberately seems to me inexcusable."

He regarded her thoughtfully. "It would seem you are a considerate person, señorita. You have a certain gentle sweetness about you. But—" He broke off abruptly.

"But what?" she prompted, then noticed his expression had grown cold.

"Gentleness and sweetness are appealing feminine characteristics, but I have found they sometimes conceal a deceitful heart."

"Señor, are you implying—" Color suffused Linda's face. "I have a feeling I remind you of someone, but I happen to be *me*, Linda Monroe."

"And who and what is Linda Monroe?" the Don asked, as though baiting her.

"You know perfectly well I can't answer that!" she snapped, making a move to rise. His hand captured her wrist, forcing her to remain seated.

"You have a temper, eh, despite that angel face. You do have the look of an angel, you know." His voice dripped cynicism.

Her chin went up. "And you don't trust angels, is that it?"

"Human angels." His gaze probed hers. "They hide all kinds of flaws beneath their innocent façades."

"Doesn't everyone have flaws?" she challenged.

"Ah, but there are those who know how to hide their imperfections. And those who—But enough of that!"

He let go of her wrist and stood up abruptly, as though disturbed by his thoughts. "I have been away from home for some days and should be going over the estate ledgers. You will excuse me." He made a formal bow and strode toward the house.

Linda remained where she was, her eyes turned toward the carved door behind which he had disappeared. How deeply he must have been wounded by some woman he had loved! But why should women in general have to bear the brunt of his mistrust?

Lowering her glance, Linda saw that her hands were curled tightly on her lap. She unclenched them, thinking life itself lacked fairness. A person wounded to the core did not pause to analyze his feelings; he simply *hurt*. More often than not, he vented that hurt upon others.

Don Diego's heartache involving someone dear to him had left its mark upon his soul. Had the woman betrayed him with another man? That, Linda felt sure, he would neither forget nor forgive—not a man like Diego Halcón y Pizarro, who was as proud as a Saracen prince and, no doubt, as unbending as a bar of steel.

She thought back to what he had said about her appearance, and the cynicism in his voice seemed to taunt her anew: *You do have the look of an angel, you know.*

She jumped to her feet, seething with indignation. She left the courtyard, heading for her room by the back way so as not to run into *him* again. He had given her a headache.

four

Linda's lunch tray had been removed and her luggage unpacked, with everything neatly stored away in the wardrobe and chest of drawers. She looked through her dresses without recognizing them, and then pulled out a top drawer of the chest.

A soft cover booklet lay on her lingerie, titled *Gems from the Bible.* With a welcome smile, Linda picked it up and stretched out on the chaise lounge. Holding the booklet close, she thought of the doubts and suspicions she had to contend with at *Casa de Halcón.* Her head was still throbbing from the last encounter with Don Diego. Surely Scripture would give her comfort.

She opened the booklet and read on the first page that the quotations were from the King James Version. *Did I choose this,* she wondered, *or did someone give it to me?* Flipping the pages, she saw many headings with Scripture verses listed beneath them. Pausing at "Discouraged," she read: "And we know that all things work together for good to them that love God, to them who are the called according to his purpose," Romans 8:28.

She meditated on it. *I'm thankful I haven't forgotten You, Lord. Does that Scripture mean You will make good come out of this tragedy in my life? Oh, please, dear God, please do that for me!*

Linda relaxed and spent the next ten minutes memorizing Romans 8:28. By the time she had absorbed it, the pulsing in her head was gone. She closed her eyes and reviewed her stay at the hospital. Thinking about Rosita rhapsodizing over Don Diego's good looks made her smile. Silly girl to romanticize him as Linda's Prince Charming. As if wealth and good looks a Prince Charming made. It took love, and Diego Halcón was not about to turn over the key to his heart to any woman.

Whoever fell in love with him would need the patience of Job, for it was probable he would require a long time before he was able to fully trust her. Linda sighed, realizing her thoughts had circled back to the Don.

I'll wash him out of my hair, that's what I'll do.

She crossed the hall to the bathroom. The water was hot and plentiful, and she shampooed her hair and enjoyed a leisurely soak in the tub. Resolutely, she kept her thoughts away from her host and found herself remembering more generalities and world affairs. Why, then, couldn't she recall her personal life? Still, she was thankful for what she did remember.

She slipped into her robe and went out to the gallery to watch the activity that had resumed now that siesta was over. Sturdy horses were being harnessed to farm carts, and hens squawked as they were shooed out of the way. Several of the men eyed Linda with interest, which she pretended not to notice.

The dog and a cock were having a friendly skirmish, with the cock trying to settle on the dog's back, only to have the dog roll on the ground. Finally, the dog permitted the bird to gain a foothold, whereupon the cock flapped his wings and crowed triumphantly as the dog treated him to a ride around the grounds.

Linda chuckled, enjoying their antics. The wolfish-looking dog was, after all, a sheep in wolf's clothing.

She sniffed the air, liking the smell of hay and horses. The valley was like a great bowl beneath the craggy sierras that wore mantles of snow even in summer. She could see a dark hawk swooping in the sky, and it reminded her of the Halcón crest. That, of course, reminded her of Don Diego, and once again he was in her thoughts.

"What is it with that man!" Linda muttered, brushing her hair with vigor, only to utter "Ouch!" as the bristles passed roughly over her tender spot.

She decided to find a book to read and went downstairs to see if there was a library. Peeking into the *sala principal,* she was impressed by its gracious air of refinement. Everything looked well-cared for and in perfect taste, from the beautiful Oriental carpet to the ruby damask of sofas and draperies. She saw lamps on black onyx bases and a fireplace tiled with colorful mosaics. Dominating one side of the room stood an ebony grand piano with Spanish scenes painted on its sides. It was supported by gilded hawks for legs.

After a brief glance into the formal dining room, Linda approached a door that stood ajar, revealing bookshelves within. She pushed the door open and found herself facing Don Diego, seated behind a large desk with an open ledger before him.

"Oh! I. . .I'm sorry if I've disturbed you," she said, flustered at this unexpected encounter. "I'm looking for a book to read."

"Come in, come in, señorita. I am finished and on my way out." He closed the ledger, slipped it into a drawer, and rose. "Volumes in English are in that corner section," he pointed out with a wave of his hand.

He made no move to leave, and Linda walked

self-consciously to the shelves he had indicated, aware that he was staring at her.

She felt rather than saw him come toward her, and she turned to face him. As he reached out his hand, she tried not to jerk away like a nervous schoolgirl.

"You washed your hair. It is very beautiful." He took a silky lock between his fingers. "The waves are natural, are they not? But the color, out of a bottle? Such golden hair is rare with dark eyes like yours."

She did not take offense. "We'll soon know if dark roots appear. But I have the complexion of a blond, wouldn't you say?"

"Many brunettes have white skin, including Castilian women of Spain." A sardonic smile touched his lips. "I shall find it interesting to observe the part in your hair."

"What does it matter whether the color is natural or not? I wouldn't like for you to be watching me, señor."

He shrugged. "Like it or not, I shall be keeping an eye on you. To make sure you rest, eat, and get well. As soon as possible," he added emphatically.

Linda's chin tilted upward. "Exactly my intention—to get well as quickly as possible. I trust my memory will return within the next couple weeks and I'll be myself again."

"*Sí,* that is what I am expecting."

"No more than I. I'm eager to go home, I assure you."

"Eager?" He pounced on the word. "But if you recall nothing of home and friends, how can you feel eager?" he demanded. "I should think you would be hesitant, even a little fearful, not knowing what to expect or what kind of life you have been living."

"By that time I'll know."

"But right now you do *not* know, you have said. Yet

you used the word 'eager.'"

Linda stared at him helplessly, feeling herself flush. It had begun, the analyzing of what came out of her mouth, the seeking for flaws that might reinforce his suspicions. Frustrated, she turned away and made a pretense of studying the titles on the bookshelves.

Silence prevailed. She pulled out a book at random and turned to leave, only to find the Don regarding her with a strange intensity that heightened her color once again.

Softly he said, "Why do you blush, señorita?"

Why, indeed? She moistened her lips. "You're staring at me, that's why."

"Are you not accustomed to being stared at? With that hair and face, any man of flesh and blood would find you pleasing to look at. And I am but a man."

Linda caught her breath and dropped her book as he stepped forward and cupped her chin with his hand, holding her so that he could look down into her face. Her heart leaped, and she could feel herself growing weak beneath his touch. Something burned in the depths of his exotic eyes, and she could see the pulse beating in his throat. He was close, so very close, this intense Spaniard. Was he going to kiss her?

Time stood still as they gazed into each other's eyes. Then his arms circled her, pulling her against him. To her dismay, a wild thrill tingled through her, an electrical response that took her breath away and turned her knees to jelly, leaving her helplessly exposed to his lips as they came down hard on hers.

It was a scorching kiss, all passion, no tenderness—a kiss that throbbed and thrilled, yet at the same time frightened her with its fierceness.

She tried to wrench away, but within those powerful arms she was as much a prisoner as though bound by steel bands, until, with a muttered exclamation, the Don thrust her from him and turned away, his hands clenched at his sides.

Linda swayed against the bookshelves, trembling all over. She stared at his rigid back, a hand pressed to her lips. His masculinity was overpowering. She had *wanted* him to kiss her.

It was a shattering thought, considering the antagonism that smoldered between them. Flesh had beckoned to flesh, although he no more wished to desire her than she did him. For a few minutes he had lost self-control. Now he regretted it.

Linda's face burned as she flew to the safety of her room. She could still feel the tingling sensation that had coursed through her body. There must have been many women in his life whenever he could get away from his responsibilities. He had admitted he was but a man of flesh and blood.

She, too, was flesh and blood. But she was not about to give her kisses away to just anyone.

How do you know what kind of girl you are, Linda Monroe? Remember what Sancho said?

"I don't care what he said! I'm a decent girl!" The protest came forth fiercely in the quiet room, so that the sound of her own voice startled her.

It took fifteen minutes of pacing the floor before Linda had calmed down enough to want to sit and read, only to realize she had dropped her book in the library.

When it came near dinner time, Linda dressed reluctantly, wishing she didn't have to face her host again.

But she couldn't go on hiding in her room. She must behave as though nothing had happened.

She selected a simple but elegant black dress and matching pumps. Her hair she left loose about her shoulders, and she doubled a long gold chain about her neck. Applying face powder and a touch of rose lipstick, she was ready.

On her way down the stairs, Linda's gaze flicked over the hanging lamps, now lit, and the graceful Moorish arches flanking the spacious hall below. Again she thought about the slave girls who must have wandered through this building at one time. The *Casa,* having been built by Moors, was so old it seemed to hint of the full gamut of human emotions.

The master of the house appeared in the hall and awaited her descent. She noted how well his white dinner jacket and narrow black trousers fit his splendid physique. She hoped he would not mention the incident in the library, and on reaching him, she seized upon a safe topic of conversation. Indicating the tapestry on the wall she said, "That scene intrigues me. I should think the dove would be fleeing the hawk. Is it your family crest?"

He nodded, explaining, "The olive tree represents the plantation, our livelihood. The hawk represents the line of Halcón males, since halcón means hawk in Spanish; and the pure white *paloma,* the women they married." He pointed toward the ancestral portraits lining the central wall of the gallery above the stairs. "There they are, the Halcóns, male and female, pictured in the prime of life—the good and the bad."

Bad? Perhaps one of the hawks had turned out to be a black sheep, Linda speculated.

"Come," the Don said. "What will you have to drink before dinner?"

"Some mineral water, señor."

"Very well." Crooking his arm, he escorted her into the main *sala.* "When my sister does not appear at this time for drinks, she comes down precisely at nine for dinner. You will find she is an exacting individual and always on time, and she expects it of others as well. Perhaps too exacting, but I cannot complain, for she sees to it that my home is kept spotless and running like a well-oiled machine. Josefa never married, and this house, you might say, is her whole life."

"Quite the perfectionist. I've sensed that already." Linda murmured.

"She manages all things pertaining to the house and servants, whereas I keep an eye on the outside work."

"Do you have overseers?" Linda asked.

"*Sí,* but it is good policy to oversee the overseers. Keeps them on their toes," Don Diego told her as he poured mineral water into glasses and handed Linda her drink.

"Your sister said you have a child living with you, a nephew. I'm looking forward to meeting him. I like children."

His hand paused in the act of lifting his glass to his lips. "And how can you know that?"

"Know what?"

"That you like children."

"Why, I don't know. It just came out. Don't most people like children? Perhaps I'm starting to remember."

Or perhaps it was a slip of the tongue. Linda could almost see the thought reflected in his eyes, and she said defiantly, "It must have come out of my subconscious mind."

"Possibly." He drained his glass and set it down. "I like children. But should I not marry, Juanito will inherit the plantation. He is like a son to me."

"So you do not feel pressured to produce an heir?"

"You could say that."

"How fortunate, considering you're in no hurry to take a wife and are so particular." Linda regretted the sarcasm the moment the words passed her lips. "I'm sorry," she said, clasping her hands and looking down at them to avoid his eyes. "That was rude of me. Please forgive me, señor."

"Ahh, there it is again."

She raised her head. "Pardon?"

"That gentle sweetness." The mocking look from narrowed eyes told her he suspected she might be putting on an act.

Always on guard, she thought, suppressing her irritation. He had no intention of taking her at face value, and whatever she said would be digested with a grain of salt. Would it help to clear the air if she told him she knew what he suspected? Or had she already waited too long? Would it make matters better or worse? She did not know, so she kept silent.

"About Juanito," he said, "you will see him tomorrow. He is spending the weekend with Francisco Ruis. Francisco is a widower with a son close to Juanito's age. The two boys get together quite often."

The dinner gong sounded, and they went out to the hall to wait for Doña Josefa. Linda walked over to the tapestry to study its intricate weavings. When she turned from it, Doña Josefa was on her way down the stairs.

She had changed from the black bombazine to a gown of gray silk with white lace at the throat, which gave a softening effect to the austere lines of her features. She smiled down at her brother, who was standing at the foot of the staircase, waiting to escort the two women into the dining room. It was evident he extended every courtesy to his sister. As she neared him, her gaze warm upon his face, it struck Linda that the Doña loved her brother dearly.

In the formal dining *sala,* brass and crystal chandeliers shed their soft light upon a long table that gleamed with silver and crystal. Carnations in a jade bowl lent spice to the air.

Don Diego seated his sister at his right, Linda at his left. As Linda unfolded her embroidered napkin, she reflected on how graciously these people lived, despite the fact that they were miles from the nearest city.

The dinner was served by a male servant. A tasty broth with croutons. Shrimp with a delicious sauce. Filets of tender beef garnished with green peppers and onions. A crisp green salad. Fresh sliced nectarines in cream.

The meal was punctuated with conversation, mostly between the brother and sister concerning the affairs of the estate. They spoke English out of deference to Linda, but it was inevitable that they would lapse occasionally into their native tongue.

During one of these lapses, Doña Josefa expressed anxiety over Linda's affliction. What were they to do should the young lady not regain her memory when her concussion healed? Her brother replied that they would worry about that when the time came. Meanwhile, he wanted the Doña to stay alert for incriminating slips of the tongue, since it was possible their angel-faced guest was not what she appeared to be.

Almost choking on her food, Linda went into a coughing spell that, if nothing else, successfully masked the fact that her scarlet face was due to anger. Afraid of what she might say or do if she remained at the table, she gulped down some water and stood up.

"Excuse me, I'd like to retire now," she said hoarsely. "My head hurts." She fled, not caring what they might think. Had she remained, she might have flung the rest of her water in Don Diego's handsome face.

five

When Linda finally fell asleep, she had a disturbing dream. She was knocking on doors and making inquiries, as though seeking someone. When she came to a door that seemed to be the right one, she approached it eagerly. Suddenly, something struck her from behind, hurling her to the ground. Her head hit the pavement— and she awoke with a cry.

The dream was still vivid while she washed and dressed. Could that be why she had come to Spain? To find someone? Since part of the dream was true—she *was* struck down—perhaps the other part was true also.

Catching her wide-eyed expression in the mirror, Linda made a face at herself. She was romanticizing her situation like Rosita, when actually she had come to this country on vacation like any other American tourist. Once memory returned and she went home, all this would seem like some fantastic adventure to share with friends and coworkers, and they would chuckle that her Spanish host could have suspected her of intrigue.

She sighed as she fastened her hair at her nape with a silver barrette. At present her situation seemed anything but humorous, especially having to conceal her understanding of Spanish. She wondered if she could also read Spanish and decided to check it out when the library was vacant.

Linda had Pepa set her breakfast on the balcony table: slices of fresh warm bread with a little dish of olive oil for dipping, scrambled eggs, a thick slab of home-cured ham, rich dark Spanish coffee, and a fresh peach.

The Andalusian morning was dressed in its finest weather, and the honeysuckle entwining the wrought-iron of the balcony generously exuded its fragrance. Several bees buzzed about the nectar-rich flowers, ignoring Linda's presence. It was a soothing place to start her day, and she drank in the tranquility while enjoying her hearty breakfast. From out back came the cooing of pigeons. A horse whinnied.

She would love to mount a horse—did she ride?— and go trotting across the countryside. Were it not for the unpleasant undercurrents, she would enjoy her stay here.

On the way downstairs, Linda paused to take a closer look at the Halcón ancestral portraits. The ladies were lovely, some wearing *mantillas* and jewelled combs in their dark hair. She could see resemblances among several of the men—the tilt of the eyes, the proud nose, the forceful jaw. Studying the faces from left to right, Linda decided the last two must be the parents of her host and hostess. Don Diego strongly resembled the man, as did Josefa. The mother had a heart-shaped face with a creamy complexion and big brown eyes fringed with long dark lashes. She wore a red rose in her hair. What tragedy had befallen that lovely woman and her husband?

When Linda reached the library, it was vacant, and she was able to take a look around. The walls were paneled, and several colorful Oriental rugs lay on the polished floor. A long table stood on one rug. Displayed on the wall between two windows was a large oil painting of a *matador* in the act of killing a bull with his sword.

Linda selected a volume from the shelves of Spanish books, flipped open the pages, and ran her gaze over the printed words. At first they looked strange to her, but then she found herself reading—not rapidly, but without difficulty.

It would seem she was a student of the Spanish language and had learned it well. She liked it, felt an affinity for it. No wonder she had come to Spain. If only she were free to communicate with the people in their own tongue, she thought wistfully.

Linda spent an hour in the library, sampling pages from Spanish, English, and American volumes. The discovery that she was a lover of books pleased her. Little by little, she was getting to know herself, even without the aid of memory.

Another pleasant hour was spent in the *sala principal,* listening to recordings. One by Andrés Segovia, the great Spanish classical guitarist, thrilled her. She loved the sound of the guitar, and her taste in music seemed to lean toward the classical and semi-classical.

She went out to the courtyard and noticed that the overhead section of the iron gates formed the name and crest of the Halcón family. She meandered among the greenery, admiring golden creepers, blue plumbago, and pink and ruby myrtles. Pausing beside the orange tree that wasn't much taller than she was, she reached out to fondle a little green globe. Such a small tree to be bearing fruit. Amazing.

Although Linda did not hear the *patrono* enter the courtyard, she sensed his presence. At once, her feeling of peace vanished. Collecting her composure around her like a cloak, she turned to face him.

"I wish you wouldn't creep up on me like that," she protested. "Really, you walk like a jungle cat."

He looked amused. "Should I growl next time to warn you of my approach? It is the only way I know to walk."

Linda guessed there was no point in pursuing the subject so she remained silent.

"You were admiring the orange tree," the Don said after a moment's quiet. "Perhaps you would like to walk through the fruit orchard? Come, I will show you."

They strolled side by side to the orchard. There were no laborers in the fields on Sunday, no voices calling out. Only the chirping of birds and the hum of bees. They went first to the citrus section where orange, grapefruit, and lemon trees grew in straight rows. Linda gazed with delight at white blossoms and abundant fruit.

"How sweet the smell of orange blossoms!" She buried her nose in a cluster of delicate, star-like petals.

The Don smiled. "You enjoy the things of nature, eh?"

"What could be more beautiful? I feel very close to the Creator here among His handiwork. Thank God I haven't forgotten Him! I assume you believe in God and an afterlife, señor?"

"I was brought up to believe, *sí*. But I have not been to church in years. Frankly, I do not spend much time thinking about God."

Because of her, Linda thought sorrowfully. That woman in his past, whoever she was, had made a cynic of him. How sad to allow old hurts to go on giving pain! Was he using that hurt as a shield? Yet everybody needed a special someone to love. It might melt Don Diego's cynicism, if he would just open up his heart.

He showed Linda peaches, nectarines, apricots, figs, and almonds. He plucked a handful of purplish figs for them to eat on their way back to the courtyard, where they seated themselves by the fountain.

"When is Juanito coming home?" Linda wanted to know. "Does he speak English?"

"He has been tutored in English. Don Francisco is bringing him home tonight and will stay for dinner."

"How long has Don Francisco been a widower?"

"Almost three years. His wife died giving birth to a stillborn child. Relatives live with him and help run his business."

"Does he grow olives?"

"He breeds livestock. A nice fellow, Francisco, but he's too soft."

"In what way?"

"He is the *dueño,* the owner and master of the ranch, yet he lets his family run him. Too easygoing—especially with his womenfolk."

"And you consider that a weakness?"

"Women are quick to take advantage of such a man."

"You feel the man must keep his womenfolk in line?"

"That does not appeal to you, eh? But this is Spain, not America where so many husbands permit themselves to be—how do you call it?—henpecked. *¡Por mi vida!* That will be the day when a woman henpecks me!"

He was the modern equivalent of those self-sufficient overlords of long ago, thought Linda. He followed the traditions of his family, ruling over his domain with an iron hand.

The Don threw Linda a narrow glance, and the mocking gleam was back in his eye. "Women are like horses, my dear señorita; they must be bridled, or they will take the lead."

"I don't appreciate being compared to a horse," said

Linda.

"Ah, but the horse is a very fine and beautiful animal, indispensable to man. The same goes for women. What man does not enjoy their beauty, their warmth, and comfort? Not to mention the fine sons they produce for their husbands."

"I get the impression you regard women as chattels, placed on earth solely for the benefit of men, and that a wife's sole duty is to please her husband and bear his sons." The flush of indignation coloring Linda's cheeks gave her the look of a wild rose.

"The liberated female in you rears up occasionally, I see," Don Diego commented. "But, then, you are a *norte americana*. The women of southern Spain think differently. They take pleasure in making their husbands happy. It is the belief of the Spanish people that a woman is the rib of the man she marries. That should tell you something."

"But what if a wife becomes a sword in her husband's side instead of a rib?"

His eyes narrowed. "How do you mean that?"

"Suppose she's unhappy in her marriage and turns to another man. I wonder, would her lord and master consider the possibility that he might not have met *her* needs? Or instead would he throw her out or even kill her?"

The Don's reaction startled Linda. Color receded from his face, and his flaming eyes burned into hers. His hands had curled into fists. Silence spun a web about them. Instinctively, Linda knew she had dredged up some horror from his past. The tension was more than she could bear.

Springing to her feet, she mumbled, "Excuse me. I

think I'll go up and change for lunch." She fled.

Luncheon turned out to be a constrained affair, with the Don so silent and withdrawn that even his sister noticed. Linda was relieved when the meal ended and they could retire to their rooms for siesta.

Why had Diego Halcón reacted so strangely? she asked herself. Such a personal reaction had to mean something. Troubled by the mystery she had discovered, Linda tossed and turned in her bed. Several minutes passed before she was able to drift off to sleep.

When she woke later that afternoon, Linda decided to look through her drawers for a handkerchief. While searching, she found a Bible with her name in it. Though she did not recognize it as her own, it was a welcome sight.

She examined the cover of black imitation leather, then held the book by its spine to see the thickness of the many pages. As she loosened her hold, the Bible fell open in her hand, and one verse seemed to leap off the page: "Never will I leave you; never will I forsake you."

"Thank You, Lord," she whispered. "I'll always need You."

Turning to the flyleaf, she read, "I, Linda Monroe, age 19, am now a born-again Christian. Hallelujah!" Linda smiled, hugged the Bible to her heart, and spent the rest of the afternoon reading the Gospel of John. The scene between Nicodemus and Jesus in chapter three made her wonder where she had accepted the Lord as her Savior.

The white gown Linda chose to wear for dinner that night had flowing Grecian lines that draped her slender body. It was a lovely dress, soft and silky, but with no label. She examined the seams and the hand-stitched hem and wondered if she had made the dress herself. It was a classic style that would probably never go out of fashion.

With it she wore white strap sandals and a simple gold bracelet. She piled her hair loosely on top of her head, leaving a wavy tendril in front of each ear. The style made her look older, she noted with satisfaction. Perhaps when she was thirty she would appreciate appearing younger than her age. But at twenty-four, it was frustrating to look like a teenager.

Linda joined the Halcóns and their guest in the main *sala*.

"What have we here, a Greek goddess?" her host said with a smile. Evidently the cloud on his spirit had lifted. He made the introductions. "Señorita, may I present Francisco Ruiz Loyola. Francisco—our American guest, Miss Linda Monroe."

"How do you do?" Linda extended her hand to the *caballero*, who was observing her with keen interest. He was medium height and very slim in his white dinner jacket. His eyes were a soft brown, warm and benign, as was his smile. Linda felt drawn to him at once.

"This is a pleasure, señorita," he murmured, bowing over her hand in the gracious continental manner. " Diego was telling me how you came to be here, but he forgot to mention how lovely you are." Like most educated Spaniards, he had good command of the English language.

"Thank you, señor." Linda smiled at him. She felt the compliment was sincere, not just a *piropo*, a flirtatious comment.

"And this is my nephew, Juanito Halcón," Don Diego said, as she turned to face the wiry, sun-bronzed youngster who resembled his uncle enough to be taken for his son. He, too, bowed over Linda's hand, the perfect little gentleman.

"*Buenas noches,* señorita," he greeted her politely. That done, he quickly shed formality and said eagerly, "You will tell me about Disney World in Florida, yes? Have you seen the figures that move and talk and sing like real people? You have been to Disney World?"

"I can't remember if I've been there, although I doubt it," Linda told him. "I guess you know I have amnesia?"

"*Tío* said you hit your head when his car knocked you down. Now you have no memory about yourself? I am sorry." Dark eyes regarded her curiously. "Still, how can anyone forget a magical place like Disney World?"

"I've heard of it, but I'm from New York, according to my passport," Linda explained. "That's a long way from Disney World in Florida. Maybe twelve hundred miles."

The boy turned to his uncle. "And what is that in kilometers, *Tío?*"

"Almost two thousand."

"Ah, a long way."

Doña Josefa, who was wearing a burgundy gown, remarked, "It seems odd that Miss Monroe knows about Disney World and the distance between New York and Florida, yet cannot remember her own hometown."

"It feels odd," Linda agreed.

"Perhaps you will remember everything soon," Juanito said cheerfully. "Then you can tell me about Disney World, if you have been there."

"Gladly. And call me Linda." She was grateful that at least one member of the Halcón family accepted her, amnesia and all.

Don Francisco drew her to where they could sit down together. "Linda." He rolled her name over his tongue caressingly. "It means pretty. A Spanish name."

"And very popular in the United States," she told him. "Many American girls are named Linda. Not all of them know it's a Spanish name or realize what it means. You raise livestock, señor?"

He nodded. "I hope you will come to see my ranch. My mother lives with me, and my sister and her family. I have a son, Manuel, who is eleven. Perhaps you know my wife died several years ago?"

"Don Diego told me. I'm so sorry."

"She was a fine woman, my Caroline, but fragile. She wanted more children after Manuel, but many years passed before she conceived again. It was a stillbirth with complications."

"It must be a comfort to have Manuel."

"Indeed. But a man needs a wife, señorita, and I have much love to give."

Looking into Francisco's clear brown eyes, Linda could feel *simpatía* flowing between them and sensed that he felt it too. If he was easygoing with his womenfolk, it was because he loved, not because he was weak, as Don Diego seemed to think. Wasn't love a matter of giving, of making the other person happy? Since when was that considered a weakness?

"May I speak to you frankly, señorita?" he was saying.

"Of course."

"I am thirty-eight years old and not a frivolous man.

But from the moment I first looked into your eyes, I knew I wanted to spend time with you and talk to you." Francisco's smile held a singular sweetness. "They say the eyes are the mirror of the soul. I believe it. Looking into your eyes, I feel I know the kind of person you are. Someone good. Someone sweet and loving. I would like to see you again, señorita. You will permit me?"

Linda stared at him, touched by the rapport between them. A kinship had sprung up almost at the moment of meeting. In Spanish, *simpatía* expressed it fairly well, and it did not necessarily involve romantic feelings. It could happen between two members of the same gender, or between a child and an elderly person. It was a kind of harmony, special warmth and liking, a feeling of, "Hey, that's my kind of person!"

"I have to admit I feel a rapport with you, Don Francisco," she told him sincerely. "I would like us to be friends, but I'll be leaving Spain before long, you know."

"That is why I decided to speak up. We Spaniards believe that what is meant to be will be. Who knows? Perhaps you will not leave Spain. But whatever comes of our meeting, I believe I will be the richer for having known you."

"What a lovely compliment!"

"You will spend a day at my ranch, *por favor?* May I pick you up, say, Tuesday morning at nine?"

"Tuesday at nine. I'll be ready."

Pleasure lit up his face. Impulsively, he reached for her hand and carried it to his lips. Out of the corner of her eye, Linda saw that the Halcóns were observing them. It must be obvious that Don Francisco was more than a little interested in her. She wondered what they were thinking.

six

Juanito sat beside Linda at the dinner table, and Don Francisco sat across from them next to Doña Josefa. During the roast lamb dinner, Juanito said something about wanting to see another *corrida de toros,* and the bullfight became the topic of discussion. Words of the trade were tossed about, and because Linda had been reading a bullfight story that very day, she understood their meaning. But whereas her Spanish companions expressed enthusiasm for the *corrida,* she felt only negative emotions and told them so quite frankly.

"I'm surprised they allow children where blood is shed. To me the whole system of bullfighting seems barbaric. It appears man will do almost anything to achieve glory—even cruelty to dumb animals. Yet Spain is a civilized country?" She left the irony dangling and jabbed with her fork at a roast potato on her plate, the gesture expressing her disapproval more than words.

"Yours is the usual American attitude," Don Diego said. "It indicates lack of understanding of the basic nature of the *corrida de toros.* I suggest you read Hemingway's *Death in the Afternoon* before you denounce our national sport. You will find it in the library."

"Since you feel as you do, señorita, I would like you to know that the bulls I raise on my ranch are sold to breeding farms, not to the arena."

"I'm glad to hear it, Don Francisco. But you do attend bullfights?"

He gestured with an expressive hand. "A few. I have to admit I admire the grace and courage of a good *matador*. But I get no enjoyment out of seeing a fine fighting bull receive the *coup de grâce*. It leaves me feeling a little sad."

Don Diego quirked an eyebrow at him. "Are you sure you are a son of Spain, *amigo*?"

Linda defended her new friend. "You seem to consider sensitivity in a man a drawback, Señor Halcón. I think it's an admirable trait, and I'm glad someone in this country of bullfights feels sympathy for the poor animals."

"Diego and I do not always see eye to eye," Don Francisco told her. "It seems I lack the so-called fiery Spanish temperament and—shall I say—streak of cruelty?" He added wryly, "To tell the truth, I do not miss those traits in the least."

With that, he changed the subject and graciously drew Doña Josefa into the conversation by asking her advice about some household problem. From there the talk went on to the price of livestock, the influx of tourists, the quality of Spanish life.

Juanito looked sleepy and was excused as soon as he had finished eating. Coffee was served and the voices of the other adults faded for Linda as she sat back and observed them.

Focusing on Don Diego's profile, she noted that every line of his face was as firmly chiselled as though carved by a sculptor. No weakness anywhere, no blurring of lines. His slim, muscular body moved so fluidly—how magnificent he would look in a *torero's* brocaded *traje de luces,* the suit of lights.

Linda pictured him as the matador of the painting in

the library, and a chill ran down her spine. She did not doubt that were he a bullfighter, he would be one of the most brave, for he gave the impression he would do all things well, forcefully, and thoroughly. As for sensitivity, if he still had any, it did not show in his strong, brooding features.

Not so Don Francisco, she thought, giving him her attention. He was talking about Juanito and Manuel and the fun they had had with the calves on his ranch. He spoke with humor and affection. There was something sweet and open about Francisco that appealed to Linda.

How dissimilar he and his friend were! The younger man's look of inborn authority and his slightly aloof bearing kept one at a distance, whereas Don Francisco radiated a warmth that made him approachable and easy to know. It wasn't difficult to picture him romping on hands and knees with his son. Linda couldn't imagine Diego Halcón romping that way, not even with a child.

Her gaze moved on to Doña Josefa. She noticed that whenever the woman remained silent for any length of time, Don Francisco made opportunity for her to be drawn into the conversation.

Had Doña Josefa always walked with a limp? Did she regret not being married and having a family of her own? Was that why she so seldom smiled and why this house and her brother meant so much to her? You could see her affection for him in the way her expression softened when she looked at him, yet there was something possessive in the way she loved him. And Juanito. She was fond of her nephew. Linda had seen her hugging him.

A plain woman, Doña Josefa evidently knew her limitations and had settled for being neat and clean and dignified, without makeup or fancy hairdos. She wore her long black hair in thick braids, like a crown, on her head. Her burgundy gown was high-necked and severe, but the color lent warmth to her sallow complexion. A cross of antique gold studded with rubies and pearls hung on a long gold chain from her neck.

"It's exquisite," Linda commented, as the Doña noticed her admiring it. The Doña explained that it was a family heirloom.

It was almost 10:30 when they arose from the table and went into the main *sala*. Linda discovered who played the piano when Don Francisco asked Doña Josefa to honor them with her musical talent. She seemed pleased that he wished to hear her play and swung into a melody so rhythmic, Linda couldn't keep her feet still. It took her by surprise, for she had expected something classical from the dignified lady at the instrument. It sounded like a dance tune, and if Doña Josefa couldn't dance on her lame leg, she certainly made up for it with her dancing fingers.

"She is playing music of 'The Angelina,' which is a ring-dance," Don Francisco explained to Linda, smiling at her tapping feet. "It is a merry dance, with rings of men and women in alternate positions. Dancing is as natural as breathing to the Spanish."

They applauded when the tune ended, and Linda made a request. "Could you play a tango for us, Doña Josefa? 'La Cumparsita'? It's my favorite tango." She paused, aware that her host and hostess had exchanged significant glances. "Now w. . .what made me say that?" she stammered.

"Memory may be returning," Don Francisco suggested.

"I hope so, but it's gone, the feeling of that being my favorite tango."

The others remained silent. Were they keeping track of possibly incriminating comments made by her? And who were they to decide what was an incriminating slip and what wasn't?

No! She wasn't going to let them spoil her evening. She made herself smile at Doña Josefa and repeat her request. She then thoroughly enjoyed the tango and thanked her for her excellent rendition.

As the evening ended, Don Francisco bowed over Linda's hand, murmuring, "*Buenas noches*—until Tuesday."

On Monday, Linda spent time with Juanito, who took her on a tour through the outbuildings. He showed her the pressing mills where the olives were crushed and briefly explained the process. He expressed regret that it wasn't the right season for her to see how it was done. The olives matured from October on and were harvested until the end of February. The best oil came from those picked just after they ripened, before they turned black. If picked too green, Juanito told her, the oil would be bitter; if picked too ripe, the oil would taste rancid. Halcón oil was always of the best quality.

"You're very knowledgeable for your age," said Linda.

He wrinkled his brow. "What does it mean, that big word?"

"Knowledgeable means you know a lot."

"My uncle, he teaches me. I do the rounds with him many times all over the estate. He wants for me to help him run it when I am older."

"Would you like that, Juanito?"

He hesitated. "I like it here and Tío needs me, but I want to be a *torero!*"

"A bullfighter? Oh, Juanito, no!"

"*Si!* To be a famous bullfighter, what could be more exciting? All of Spain admires such a brave man. You should see at least one bullfight before you go home, Linda." The Spanish pronunciation of her name—Leenda—gave it a musical sound.

"Is your uncle aware of this ambition of yours, Juanito?"

"I mentioned it. He said all Spanish boys dream of becoming *toreros*, but with most that is all it is, a dream. I think not with me, and I will talk to him again about it."

"Have you seen many bullfights?"

"Quite a few. Mostly in Seville and one in Madrid. Madrid is where you see the most famous *toreros*. Seville is the second most important place for bullfights."

"Doesn't it bother you, the gorings and the blood?"

"The first time or two." He shrugged. "I am used to it now. Listen, Linda, the bullfight is very exciting when you understand it. I have read all about the passes with the cape and how they should be done and what makes a *torero* great. It takes a very brave man to work the cape really close to the bull, and the closer he lets the bull come, the more dangerous it is."

And the more dangerous, the more the crowds love it, thought Linda. Only a cruel people could enjoy such a spectacle. This Spanish attitude toward the bullfight evidently was acquired at an early age. Already this twelve-year-old took for granted the spilling of blood and the senseless slaughter of animals for no better reason than to be thrilled by daredeviltry.

Perhaps she should take Don Diego's suggestion and read Hemingway's *Death in the Afternoon.* It might explain to her the Spanish mentality that took pleasure in so brutal a drama as the *corrida de toros,* which literally meant "the running of the bulls."

If Juanito followed through on his desire to be a bullfighter, the vast Halcón estate would be left without an heir and Don Diego would be compelled to take a wife. As the head of a family that had gone on for hundreds of years, he certainly would not permit his empire to fall into the hands of strangers. Did Juanito truly understand the legacy?

His next words gave her the answer. "*Tía* Josefa does not want me ever to leave here. She does not think my uncle will marry, and in that case I would inherit his property. But I would have to stay here to run it. I would rather be a *torero,* like the popular ones I have been reading about. Manolete, for example. He died many years ago, but Spain has not forgotten him. I intend to go to bullfighting school, perhaps next year when I turn thirteen."

"So soon? You're that serious about it?"

"Very serious. Uncle is my guardian until I grow up, but he will let me go. And he will be proud of me, for he is a great *aficionado* of the *corrida.*" Juanito shooed some chickens out of their way as they walked toward the house. "One of my relatives was a bullfighter," he went on. "A cousin of my mother. He died of tuberculosis before I was born, so I never knew him. They say he was brave, although not great. I want to be great, the best. Say, Linda, can you ride a horse?"

"Hmm, I wonder. . . ." She crinkled her brow, trying to remember.

"Want to try? We could ride to the village. It is not far."

"I'd love to, Juanito, but I'm not supposed to do any

bouncing that could affect my head."

"But if you know how to ride, you will move as one with the horse and it will not jar you."

She was tempted and looked it, so Juanito pressed the point. "We have a filly that is very gentle, and I promise we will not gallop. If you feel shaken we will quit, yes?"

"Sold!"

"The filly, she is not for sale, Linda."

She laughed. "I used the word in the sense of meaning okay, you win, I give in," she explained.

"Ah, *bien*. You are good sport. Except about the *corrida*, eh? You have clothes for riding?"

"I'll wear my jeans. Are you sure your uncle won't mind my using the horse?"

"Why should he mind? It is good exercise for her. I will lend you a hat for the sun."

Ten minutes later they were in the stable. Most of the stalls were vacant, for the work animals were out in the fields. Juanito pointed to a sleek, honey-colored horse munching oats,who turned her head to cock an eye at them as they paused by her stall.

"This is Dulzura, the filly you will ride, Linda. Her name means sweetness. The mare in the stall next to her is my horse, Castaña. Her name means chestnut."

The groom prepared the two horses for riding and led them out to the mounting block, where Linda climbed onto Dulzura's saddle. Juanito mounted and walked his chestnut around to the front of the *Casa*. Linda's horse followed. They broke into a slow, even canter that took them to the road leading into Halcón village. Linda discovered she was sitting her horse well and that her body had adapted to Dulzura's movements in perfect rhythm.

"Oh, this is wonderful!" she cried. "I must have

ridden before; it isn't jarring me."

Juanito grinned at her, and she thought how cute he looked in his black, broad-brimmed *cordobes* secured with a cord under his chin. The hat she wore was of straw. She had forgotten to put on her sunglasses and was grateful for the shade from the hat's brim.

As they passed the planted fields, several of the field hands waved to them, and they waved back. Juanito pointed out his uncle on horseback in the distance, and he, too, saw them and waved.

At the village, they tied their mounts to a hitching post in the square. Juanito warned the little boys playing there to keep their distance from the horses' hoofs. Two women standing near the public fountain stared at Linda. She gave them a smile and they smiled in return. She knew they would be whispering about her as soon as she turned her back.

Juanito took Linda exploring along cobblestone lanes set with rows of little whitewashed houses and stores that sparkled in the sun. They were ancient buildings steeped in history, and again Linda had that curious feeling of being in another world, in another time, so that her jeans seemed flagrantly out of place. She felt sure the folks behind these thick adobe walls lived their lives in the traditions of their ancestors.

No brainwashing television shows and commercials here. The fast-paced modern world had yet to influence this *pueblo* of southern Spain. The people still followed conservative customs, manners, and dress, and since their transportation was still the donkey and mule, the world had not shrunk for them as it had for others who traveled by car and plane.

"Let us go in here." Juanito paused before a tiny store with small panes of glass in its single window. "I brought some money with me."

A bell jangled as they opened the door. Spicy odors greeted them. Bundles of dried herbs hung from a beam, and bins held potatoes, onions, garlic, almonds, and pistachio nuts. On shelves stood tantalizing jars of spices and sticks of cinnamon, pickled watermelon rinds, and olives. In a glass case were squares of almond nougat, chocolates wrapped in colored foil, and other sweets.

The old proprietress put down her mending and came forward, her jet black eyes taking in Linda's appearance from head to toe. She spoke to Juanito in Spanish as he selected candies and pistachios. Linda turned her face away, pretending to examine a coffee grinder as the woman remarked on the *norte americana's* loss of memory. She would pray for the poor girl.

As they left the store, Linda smiled at the woman, reflecting wryly on the speed with which news traveled, even in the country.

Juanito handed her a foil-wrapped chocolate shaped like a fish and unwrapped a chocolate bull for himself. The sweets made them thirsty, so they stopped at a café and had Cokes at an outdoor table beneath an awning. The few people they saw were either too old or too young to work in the fields or were mothers with little ones to care for.

From Juanito, Linda learned that the town hall also served as police headquarters, and that there was one doctor and a pharmacy, but no hospital. School held one room for boys and one room for girls. All grades were taught by the two teachers. Juanito was taught at home by a private tutor from Seville who lived at the *Casa* during school sessions.

The men would be coming home soon for lunch and siesta, Juanito informed Linda, glancing at his wristwatch. At 3:30 they would return to the fields and outbuildings and work until seven. In the evening, they went to the café for a cup of coffee and to play cards or just talk with friends. They were simple, hard-working people who seemed content with their lot.

Listening to Juanito, Linda was impressed with his intelligence. His fertile mind picked up and retained everything that went on about him. No wonder his uncle had begun training him on the affairs of the plantation.

Would it be a great disappointment to him if Juanito went off to be a bullfighter? Surely, deep down in his heart, Don Diego longed for a son of his own to carry on the legacy. Linda could not believe so virile a man would choose to live his life without a wife and family of his own, no matter what in his past had soured him. Somewhere, there was a woman just right for Diego Halcón y Pizarro, and one of these days he would find her.

Upon returning to the house, Linda washed her hands and put on a dress. Having noticed a split at the tip of her right index fingernail, she searched in vain through her drawers for a nail clipper.

Perhaps Pepa had overlooked it when unpacking the luggage. Linda pulled out her brown vinyl bag from the wardrobe. Sure enough, the nail clipper was in the corner of one of the pockets.

She took care of the fingernail, then checked the other pocket as well. In it was a plain white handkerchief. It felt heavy in her hand. Something hard was concealed within the folds.

The heirloom cross!

Linda froze, unable to think as she stared numbly at the valuable piece of jewelry. Her heart performed gymnastics of fear.

She stumbled to the bed and dropped the cross upon the spread. She sank down beside it, a hand at her throat. The rubies seemed to wink at her slyly as ugly thoughts welled up like murky waters.

Last night I admired it. Is that what gave Doña Josefa the idea of planting it in my room? It had to be her—who else? My being here disturbs her, and this is a deliberate attempt to get rid of me by branding me a thief. But why? Why!

Though, like her brother, the Doña might suspect Linda of dramatizing her amnesia, that hardly seemed a reason for anything this drastic. There had to be a stronger motive.

Linda recalled the first time Doña Josefa had laid eyes on her. The very sight of her had alarmed the woman. Whatever the reason for the Doña's fears, Linda wasn't going to let her get away with this scheme.

A grim smile hovered on Linda's lips as she conceived a daring bit of irony. Balling the handkerchief in her fist with the treasure enclosed, she hastened to the right wing corridor, parallel to hers, where the family bedrooms were located.

Which was the Doña's room?

What if I'm caught in there?

She would hand her the cross, look her straight in the eye, and say, "I found this concealed in my room. Have you any idea who would do such a terrible thing, Doña Josefa?"

And then I'll turn and walk away before she can open her mouth. And she'll know that I know.

Listening at the doors along the corridor, Linda heard Juanito call out something to his uncle and the Don's voice replying from an adjoining room.

She moved on down to another door and tapped

lightly. Hearing nothing, she turned the knob and glanced in. It appeared to be a woman's room. She slipped inside and closed the door softly behind her.

She checked the wardrobe. Yes, this was Josefa's room.

Linda spread out the handkerchief on the dressing table and placed the cross and chain neatly in the center. She then checked to make sure the corridor was clear and tiptoed away, resisting the strong urge to run.

Reaction set in as soon as she was safe behind her own door, and she sagged against it, trembling. When she had composed herself, Linda reclined on the chaise lounge and awaited the inevitable confrontation. The knock on her door came within ten minutes. *Doña Josefa is wasting no time,* Linda thought grimly.

"Come in," she called.

As the door opened and closed, she saw that the mistress of the house had brought a manservant along as a witness to what she expected to find.

Doña Josefa came to the point at once. "My heirloom cross is missing. I wish to search your room, Miss Monroe."

Linda rose from the chaise, feigning surprised indignation. "Are you accusing me of theft?"

"I simply want to look through your things. What I find or do not find will speak for itself."

"I trust you have checked out the servants' quarters before coming here?"

"The servants have been with us for years and are honest and faithful," Doña Josefa retorted. "Not one of them has ever taken anything from this house."

An icy calm enfolded Linda. Tilting her chin, she said coolly, "Search away, if it pleases you. I'm sure you'll not find your jewelry here." And she sat down to watch.

The manservant seemed uncomfortable and avoided looking directly at her. He remained near the door, his eyes on his mistress as she made a pretense of going through the drawers and then the pockets of Linda's clothes in the wardrobe. She even looked under the pillows and lifted the skirt of the bedspread to feel with her hand beneath the edges of the mattress.

Then, as if it had just occurred to her, she went to the wardrobe and pulled out the empty suitcases. As she double-checked the pockets, the older woman bit her lip. Linda knew it must have been a struggle for her to keep her face expressionless.

Without meeting Linda's eyes, and no doubt mostly for the servant's benefit, the Doña said, "It seems I owe you an apology, Miss Monroe."

"It does seem so," Linda agreed. She added, with a slight edge to her voice, "You probably misplaced it in your room somewhere, don't you think? I suggest you take another look."

Doña Josefa had the grace to blush, and she left rather hurriedly. Linda suspected the woman would order the servant not to mention the incident to his fellow workers. The Doña certainly wouldn't want her brother to know about it. Her devious plot had backfired, and when she found the cross on her dressing table, she would know that she had been outwitted.

Linda let out a long sigh, deflated of triumph. She had won this round, but it could only result in more hostility. *I must try not to antagonize her.*

seven

Linda awakened early on Tuesday with a pleasant feeling of anticipation. Don Francisco was coming for her.

After a leisurely breakfast and shower, she slipped into a cool green dress with a demure white collar and a matching green headband. Studying the girlish reflection in the dressing table mirror, she realized she no longer felt detached from it. Her mind and body had made a friendly connection, thanks to the looking glass.

She was on the verandah when Don Francisco pulled into the courtyard, driving a tan and yellow station wagon. He got out of the car looking casual in charcoal trousers and a gray, short-sleeved shirt open at the collar. *He looks more like a poet than a rancher,* Linda thought, and had to smile, for she had no idea what a poet was supposed to look like.

"*Buenos dias.* What amazing punctuality for a woman!" He came toward her as she stepped down from the verandah and took both her hands. "If I said you put the flowers to shame, would you believe me?"

She laughed and shook her head. "Say it anyway."

"You are a night-blooming jasmine, I think."

"Why that flower?"

"It is a delicate flower that slumbers during the day. But come evening, it unfurls its white petals into starlike shapes, with a fragrance of such sweetness as to be almost intoxicating." He flicked Linda's cheek with a gentle finger. "You, *chiquita,* will not grow old quickly.

81

You have the kind of beauty that will slumber until you are thirty. Ah, then begins full bloom. It was like that with Elizabeth Taylor, the movie star. She became a true beauty only after the sweet girlish look graduated into the mystique of maturity."

Linda smiled at his eloquence. Perhaps he did have the soul of a poet. And comparing her to a movie star yet! She looked away from him shyly.

"Come, my family is looking forward to meeting you." He handed her into the car and got in behind the wheel. "There is much curiosity, of course, about your memory loss. You will not let it distress you if they ask questions?"

"I don't mind. It's only when people doubt me—" She broke off, biting her lip.

His sidelong glance was keen as he steered the station wagon around the fountain and out of the courtyard. He did not pry, merely reached out to press her hand. The gesture told her he knew something was amiss and would stand by her should she need a friend. It lightened her heart considerably. How easy it was to relax with this man, knowing he harbored no negative feelings toward her.

"How long does it take to get to your ranch?" she asked him.

"About twenty minutes."

Soon they left Halcón territory behind, the wheels of the station wagon scattering the red dust of the road that cut through the plains. Linda saw jade cactus, giant aloes in bloom with small yellow flowers, and strange rocks sculptured by winds. They passed a village where a church loomed above simple white houses. Women were washing clothes in a stream while their children played nearby. In the distance stood the ruins of a

Moorish castle.

"Already I'm beginning to love southern Spain," Linda told her companion. "It's so open and picturesque, with nothing artificial to spoil the scenery, from what I've observed so far. I think I must be a lover of nature at heart, since all this appeals to me so much."

"I am glad," Don Francisco said. "I hope Andalusia wins your heart so that you will never want to leave." His look imparted more than his words, and a faint flush stole into Linda's cheeks. Don Diego's face flashed across her mind's eye.

"In Andalusia many things remain unchanged," Don Francisco said. "Perhaps that is part of its charm."

"Yes. But when it comes to Andalusian attitudes, a bit of broadening wouldn't hurt. It's the twentieth century, after all."

"I take it you are referring to Diego's attitude toward women?"

"His and that of other Spanish men who cling to tradition. And you, Don Francisco? What are your views on the subject?"

"Diego and I differ in many ways, señorita, but I must say I respect and admire the man. He is strong in character, a fine person in his own way. About women, yes, he is inclined to hold narrow views due to. . .certain circumstances in his life. As for marriage, many Spaniards feel their wives should be satisfied to have a home, husband, and children with a roof over her head, clothes on her back, food on the table, and security—what more can she want?"

Don Francisco smiled at Linda. "They forget that besides being a wife, a woman is an individual with a mind of her own. In the marriage vows, the Latin man tends to focus on the woman's promise to obey and overlooks his own promise to cherish her. To my way of thinking, the man who cherishes his wife will be as much concerned for her happiness as his own.

"My Caroline, for example, every now and then felt the need to get away from the ranch and have a day on her own to do as she pleased. She would drive into Seville, have lunch somewhere, go to the park, visit her married English girl friend, shop, whatever she felt like doing. She would stay overnight with her friend and return home the next day refreshed.

"And do you know," he flashed a boyish grin at Linda, "I got twice as much loving when she returned home. In making her happy, I myself reaped happiness."

"It sounds like a wonderful marriage."

"*Sí*. I am convinced unselfish love can breach any gap, señorita. My wife was reared in a different culture. When differences arose between us, we discussed them with respect for each other's opinions. When we could not reach a compromise—which was rare—Caroline bowed to my wishes as head of the home, and that is as it should be.

"Tyranny breeds discontent, whereas love begets love. No wonder Jesus commanded that we love others as ourselves. Why, love alone could cure all the problems of the world. There would be no wars, no stealing or cheating, no murders, no adultery. What a wonderful world it would be, eh, señorita?"

"Heavenly. And, please, let's not be so formal. Call me Linda."

They smiled at each other, and she wished she could fall in love with him. What a dear person he was, and how tragic that he had lost his wife so early in life! He was truly sensitive toward the feelings of others, a rare individual. The woman he married would be fortunate indeed.

"We are almost at the ranch," he said.

"Tell me about your family. Besides Manuel, you said your mother lives with you, and your sister and her family. Do they speak English?"

"All except my mother, although she understands it. She has been a widow for many years. My sister keeps house for me. She has a seventeen-year-old daughter who cannot wait for her future husband to come and carry her off—romantic child!—and an eighteen-year-old son who works with my *vaqueros,* the bull herders. My brother-in-law is foreman of the ranch, and I keep the accounts. I have two other sisters, married and living some distance from here. No brothers. There, Linda, my property is just ahead."

They had reached the grasslands where his bulls grazed. A group of calves went pounding past the car, making a primitive picture in the golden sunshine. They drove through acres of pasture where full-grown bulls stood about in groups, looking peaceful and content.

"The bull is perhaps the most courageous animal there is," Francisco informed Linda. "Especially in the arena. He is afraid of nothing. But I am glad the ones I breed will not die by the sword."

They passed bull herders mounted on horses, and two men riding together came galloping toward Linda's side of the station wagon.

"My brother-in-law and his son," Francisco said, stepping on the brake. "They want to meet the American girl."

Linda rolled down her window as the riders reined in their mounts alongside the car and swept off their broad-brimmed hats respectfully. Francisco introduced them. The stocky, middle-aged man was Pedro Boira, and his son's name was Fernando. They greeted Linda, and the older man told her they would be looking forward to having lunch with her. She thanked him, and the car pulled away.

It purred past a bunkhouse, where the bull herders lodged, and the corrals and feed sheds before stopping in front of the one-story ranch house with its white walls and red roof of arched tiles. The house was built around a central courtyard, and as the car pulled in, a boy and a teen-aged girl came running to meet them.

The girl wore a peasant-style embroidered blouse and skirt and leather sandals. She was slender and pretty with masses of wavy black hair cascading down her back. Her dark eyes shone with lively interest as Linda stepped out of the car.

"So, you are Linda Monroe!" she said, without waiting for introductions. "Uncle said you were pretty. How true! I am Mariana Boira and so glad I am you came, Linda." She gave her a quick hug.

"Why, thank you. I'm glad to be here." Linda was touched by the girl's warm welcome.

"Mariana has been dying to meet you," her uncle said with a laugh. He placed a hand on his son's head. "This is my boy, Manuel."

"Hello, Manuel." Linda saw that his eyes were blue. He gave her a shy smile.

Mariana linked arms with her as they walked to one of the doors leading into the house from the verandah. The young girl was far from reticent, and a flood of words poured from her lips.

"About losing memory, Linda, this I am sorry, and I hope everything comes back to you soon. Southern Spain, you like? Is hot, eh? Careful that white skin, our *sol* will cook it. I wonder, you find our country life boring? For me, I cannot wait to get married and live in the city. Is too isolated out here in the valley, and I do not get visits much with girls my age. Come to my room later and talk with me, yes? I wish you had not to leave after lunch."

"Perhaps I'll come again," Linda said, smiling at the way the teenager ran on without pause. She was bubbling over with youthful exuberance, and speaking in English seemed not to hinder her. Linda could just imagine how rapidly her vocabulary must flow in her native tongue.

"I know I talk much when excited," Mariana admitted, as though in answer to Linda's thoughts. "But I just *love* when company comes! We will—how you say?—chitchat later, just you and me."

They went into the living room where Francisco's sister and mother awaited them. Both women were short and plump with round faces and soft dark eyes. They, too, greeted Linda warmly, and the older woman embraced her murmuring, *"Es muy bonita, pobre niña,"* expressing sympathy over what had happened to her, as well as complimenting her looks.

"My dear child, how nice to have you with us!" Señora Boira clasped her hand and kissed her on the cheek. She instructed her daughter to ring for refreshments, then led Linda to the sofa. "We were shocked when Francisco told us what happened to you and that you remember nothing of your life. I am so sorry. We have been praying for you."

"I appreciate that." And because they all seemed genuinely concerned, Linda went on to tell of her hospital experience, of how alone and frightened she had felt, of the information in her passport, and of Don Diego's determination to look after her until she was well. She confessed remembering generalities, and that a flash had come to her briefly about "La Cumparsita," which she hoped meant she'd be regaining her personal memories soon. They listened sympathetically, murmuring words of encouragement, making her feel she was among friends.

After cool drinks served with sweet biscuits, Mariana took Linda to her room whose walls were decorated with colorful posters of bullfighters and flamenco dancers. They made themselves comfortable on the bed.

"Linda, you will not think me"—she groped for the right word—"insensitive I say something? The amnesia is *triste,* sad, of course. It must be terrible to not remember one's life and loved ones. And yet, is it not romantic, the situation? Don Diego so rich and handsome, and you so pretty. *¿Quién sabe?* My uncle he seems very interested in you, too. Maybe you will marry one or the other and make Andalusia your home." She added with Spanish fatalism, "That must be why the accident—to change the course of your life."

"You remind me of my nurse at the hospital," Linda said, laughing. "Is that all you Spanish girls think about? Romance and marriage?"

"What could be more important! Every Spanish girl expects to marry. I wonder what it is like to be kissed. Ooh, I get goose bumps just thinking about being in a man's arms!" Mariana shivered with delightful anticipation. "Does it make you feel your bones are melting? Send fire through the blood, like in the love stories? You must know, Linda. What is it like to be kissed? Tell me."

"I'm twenty-four, so I assume I've been kissed before coming to Spain, although I don't remember," Linda said. And then she recalled Don Diego's passionate kiss. "It could be like in the love stories," she added, "but passion is a physical reaction that can ignite without love. Remember that, Mariana. Lovemaking is for marriage."

Eyes sparkling, Mariana confided, "Saturday last, Papá and Mamá and I went to Seville to shop and visit the de Falla family. The son, Pablo, he has twenty-seven years and is an architect like his papa and grandpa before him. Pablo he treats me like a child. Except this last time. We had not seen each other in months, and he looked at me as if seeing me for the first time."

She smiled to herself. "I think suddenly it strike him that I am a young lady now. Oh, I like him so much, Linda! Last night I dreamed he took me in his arms and was about to kiss me—when I woke up!" Her voice expressed her disappointment.

Linda couldn't help laughing.

"Is that your ambition then, Mariana, to be a wife?"

"*Sí*, and to have my husband adore me even after I have children and grow plump. I will practice such *gracia*, the plumpness will not matter much. *Gracia*— charm, charisma—this is more important than beauty. When beauty she fades, *gracia* can hold a man's devotion to his woman.

"Is true, Linda. This I see in Mamá. I think Papá loves her more each day that passes. She is truly his rib. I hope I am Pablo's rib. I just know I could fall crazy with him. Uh, crazy in love—that is how you say? He will be here on Sunday. Come and meet him. We are having a party."

It seemed to Linda a quaint idea that a woman was the rib of the man she married. Yet it sounded biblical, for Eve was created from Adam's rib. *Whose rib am I?* she thought whimsically.

"Don Diego must be very particular *hombre* to be a bachelor still," Mariana ran on. "Hmm, could be you are meant to be his rib, Linda."

Linda felt her face grow warm at the thought.

"Ah, you blush!" Mariana's grin was saucy. "You are attracted to him, I bet. He is magnetic, yes? *Mucho hombre*—much man. Ah, Linda, why you turn so red? Can you be in love with this man and not know it? Oh, romance is so exciting!" Mariana leaped from the bed to whirl in a pirouette.

"I'm afraid you're letting your imagination run away with you," Linda said, a bit stiffly. "I'm not in love with Don Diego, nor he with me. Just because I'm staying under his roof—really now!"

Mariana flopped down on the bed again. "You are not one of those women who thinks career more important than marriage, are you? Or maybe you fear the Spanish male because he is master of his home? Yes, Don Diego, he is the kind who will own the woman he marries, from her head to her toes. But, Linda, she will like it! One can sense he is a man of fire. Do you not feel it when you are near him? Ah, you do not wish to love such a masterful man, eh? But if you are his rib, it will happen."

"You think it's inevitable?" Linda tried to speak lightly. "Surely I have some control over my future." She stood up. "I think we should join the others now."

Mariana sprang up and squeezed her hand. "Do not mind me, Linda. I want us to be friends, *sí*?"

Linda's lips relaxed into a smile. Despite being outspoken, the girl had the charm of an affectionate kitten. But all this talk about Linda being Don Diego's rib and in love with him without knowing it—preposterous! Mariana was as bad as Rosita when it came to romantic imaginings.

When Francisco took Linda on a tour of the house, he showed her a framed photograph of Caroline on his dresser. Linda saw the same blue eyes as Manuel's. The English girl had been blond and fair, with a bright, intelligent look.

Lunch was a pleasant family affair. Linda was plied with food: cold *gazpacho*, omelette filled with meat and vegetables, and home-baked bread. For dessert they had Manchego cheese with *membrillo*, a grainy, gelatin-like dish made of quince.

Conversation ranged from soccer to sightseeing in Seville and settled on the get-together for friends that was being planned for the coming Sunday. There would be a buffet supper and music, and Linda was urged to come with the Halcóns. She accepted the invitation with pleasure. When the conversation ended, it was siesta time.

During the ride back to *Casa de Halcón*, Francisco expressed satisfaction at the way his relatives had taken Linda to their hearts. She liked them too, Linda said, and was looking forward to her next visit.

"To tell the truth, I feel more at home with you and your relatives than with the Halcóns," she confessed. "They're so warm-hearted. They made me feel so welcome."

"Do you not feel welcome at *Casa de Halcón*, señorita?"

"Linda," she reminded him. "Don Diego is doing all he can for me, of course. But he feels obligated to have me there, and I can't help being aware of that."

"I would like to say you are welcome to stay at my house, Linda, but I hesitate to interfere in Diego's business."

"Nor would I want him to know I complained to you," she said.

"I would not call it complaining. But I would like to know if things become too uncomfortable for you. I am your friend, remember."

"Thank you, Francisco."

Upon arriving at the *Casa*, Linda went directly to her room. The household slept. Soon she also fell asleep.

Later, while she was listening to music, a servant brought Linda a letter that had come in the mail. The name on the upper corner of the envelope made her swallow nervously. It was with misgivings that she withdrew a note written in Spanish.

> *Dear Linda,*
> *I cannot get you out of my mind. You must let me see you again. Please! I have made inquiries and know that you will be in Seville next Monday morning for a medical checkup. Can we meet that day and spend the siesta together? Surely you can arrange it. I shall await your quick reply.*
>
> > *Be kind to me, darling.*
> > *Sancho*

What presumption! Linda refolded the note and slipped it into the envelope, determined to ignore it.

She deliberately blanked him out of her mind—there were enough complications in her life as it was—and turned her attention back to her music.

That evening, after not having seen the Halcóns all day, Linda joined them in the main *sala* shortly before the evening meal. They were quietly listening to the opera *Carmen.*

Doña Josefa was occupying the chair Linda had sat in earlier. A minute or two later, Linda saw her shift her position and reach down to retrieve something lodged between the cushion and the arm of the chair.

"Oh, I believe that's mine." Linda rose from the sofa and approached the Doña with outstretched hand. She had forgotten all about Sancho's letter.

Doña Josefa's quick glance took in the name on the upper left-hand corner before handing her the envelope. Then, as if to get back at Linda for having made a fool of her the day before, she commented slyly, "Sancho Torre from Seville. You must have gotten to know this man quite well in that one day before your accident." She cast a sidelong glance at her brother.

Disdaining to reply, Linda sat down and proceeded to rip both the letter and the envelope which she then tossed into a nearby wastebasket. She smiled at the Don and said, "I'm starved, aren't you?" And as the gong sounded, "Ah, saved by the gong!"

The smile still hovered about her lips as they went in to dine. She had handled herself quite well, she thought, and gave herself a mental pat on the back.

Before retiring, Linda went out to the courtyard. It was a bright moonlit night with a cool breeze. She paused to look at the sky. The moon, so round and golden, made her think of a brooch pinned to purple-blue velvet, and the stars were diamonds scattered by the lavish hand of God. What a fantastic Creator!

She was in a dreamy mood, loving the beauty around her, the Moorish arches of the arcade supported by columns, the flower-draped walls, the colorful tiles of the *patio* that were cleaned daily. The amber light of the fountain gilded the statuary and the cascading waters. Except for the sounds of night creatures, all was quiet and serene, and Linda felt she was in a garden paradise.

She heard someone clear his throat and knew the Don was announcing his presence so as not to startle her. She turned and watched him come toward her, a lithe and graceful figure in his black and white dinner attire. The moonlight and nearby lamp revealed him clearly.

"I love your beautiful garden," she told him. "It's the first time I've been out here after dark. Your home is like something out of the *Arabian Nights*, a historic showplace with a mystique all its own."

"I am pleased you are enjoying it. I only wish Juanito felt that way." A crease appeared between his eyebrows. "He is young, of course, but he is on fire to be a bull-fighter."

"I know."

"Did you notice how he maneuvered the conversation at the table tonight? Always the bullfight, his favorite subject. Perhaps it is his way of telling me his ambition is firm, not just a boyish dream. He has been studying my books on the subject and already knows much about it. I am afraid I may lose him by the time he is thirteen. I have been closing my eyes to it."

"Isn't thirteen young to begin such training?"

"Some start even younger. Juanito has been practicing with the calves at Don Francisco's ranch, and I have seen him doing passes with an old cape before the mirror to attain grace. I can no longer deny that the boy is serious."

"What about his academic studies?"

"I will make arrangements for that."

"How long does it take to become a full *matador*?"

"A novice spends six or seven years in training."

"That long!"

Don Diego nodded.

"And you will be left without an heir," Linda said softly. "But perhaps marriage and a son of your own are in store for you. It may be you have a rib somewhere waiting to be claimed." She spoke this last in a light tone, but immediately she recalled what Mariana had said, and her heart paused.

Standing so close to Don Diego, Linda felt a strange yearning sweep over her. Their glances locked, and she knew he was feeling something, too, for his eyes were beginning to smolder.

Catching her by the shoulders, he muttered, "What are you really like behind that angelic face, Linda Monroe? I would give anything to know!" Abruptly his mouth came down on hers.

Linda's fear melted away. Her arms slid up around his neck and her lips returned his kiss with an abandon she hadn't dreamed possible.

As suddenly as he had caught her, he let her go. Without a word, he turned on his heel and left her, and with sinking heart, she watched him stride into the house.

Something caught her eye.

Glancing up, she saw a gaunt form standing on the second floor gallery. The rigid stance of the figure expressed strong disapproval. Doña Josefa had been spying on them!

eight

Linda spent the night haunted by Don Diego. She dreamed that after the passionate kiss in the garden he had become tender, whispering in her ear that she was the rib he wanted for his own. Over and over, the dream kept repeating itself. Her pounding heart woke Linda, and she sat up with a start.

That dream—pure fantasy, of course—had been brought on by the talk of ribs, the romantic notions of both Rosita and Mariana. She sighed wearily, rang for breakfast in bed, and dozed until it came.

While eating, Linda meditated on the persistent dream. Could it be a reflection of a subconscious desire? The Don was remarkably attractive. He was also arrogant. When she married, it would be to a man who truly loved her, someone tender and considerate. Such love could surmount wide cultural differences, as it had for Francisco and his English bride.

Although Diego Halcón undoubtedly would feel passion for his bride, he would not be able to love without reservation until he learned to trust her. It might take a long time before he was willing to concede that not all angelic-looking women were of one mold. Either the blinders must fall from his eyes and heart before he wed, or he had better marry a woman who cared enough to be patient and loving no matter how long it took for him to totally surrender his heart to her.

It couldn't be me, Linda mused as she sipped her coffee. The man wouldn't think of selecting her for his lifetime dove. What did they have in common? Then, too, her peculiar situation stood between them, keeping him on guard when with her. To him, she was a possible adversary.

Well, she'd fix that. She would go home when scheduled, whether she regained her memory or not. That ought to show him she was no gold digger. She would accept a fair settlement and sign a paper to that effect, releasing him from any further obligation. Let him feel ashamed of himself for being so wrong about her.

The decision to leave made, Linda tried to ignore the heaviness that fell on her spirit.

After the incident in the courtyard garden, Linda shrank from the thought of sitting at the luncheon table with the Halcóns. She needed time to pull herself together. She donned her robe and slippers, and when Pepa returned to make her bed and pick up her breakfast things, she requested lunch upstairs as well.

When the girl had gone, Linda quietly opened her door to the corridor and moved furtively to the head of the stairs. Seeing no one in the hall below, she made her way to the library, found Hemingway's *Death in the Afternoon,* and hastened back to her room.

Making herself comfortable on the chaise lounge, she read the morning away and continued reading after lunch, both fascinated and repelled by Hemingway's detailed revelations. He had spent much time in Spain and had made a study of the *corrida de toros* which literally translated meant, "running of the bulls." His book revealed everything—not only the spectacle itself, but the various techniques of *toreros* and the kind of lives they lived and the deaths they died.

He also described the characteristics of different kinds of bulls and how they were bred, and even something of the character of the Spanish people in general that enabled them to accept death in the afternoon when executed skillfully by a brave *matador*. The greatest of Spanish national virtues was courage, and this explained the popularity of the bullfight, an ordeal of courage.

Linda found the volume frank, interesting, and informative. So informative, in fact, that by the time she turned the last page, she was not only educated on the subject of Spain's most popular spectacle, but was more fervently opposed to it than before.

Oh, yes, the bullfight was exciting, Linda had to admit, once she understood the proceedings, the fine points of the *torero's* art, and how to distinguish between poor and excellent performances. She could understand that. And, yes, there was beauty of movements that made the performance a kind of ballet. It took tremendous courage, but, oh, the cruelty of it all!

Violent death hovered constantly over the bullring, death for the animal and sometimes for the man. A number of Spain's bravest matadors had died of their *cornadas,* some in the prime of life. *What a waste!* thought Linda. In truth, the bullfight was a dramatic tragedy, something she could not endorse. At least now she could discuss the subject intelligently, should it come up again.

Her eyelids felt heavy after reading for hours. She closed them and dozed for a half hour. Then she sprang up from the chaise lounge, feeling a need to get out of her room. She had made a prisoner of herself all day, and the walls were beginning to close in on her.

She showered—the water was skimpy—and donned a long, full, silky skirt splashed with small, multi-colored flowers on a black background. She slipped on a black shell in the same soft material with a boat neck-line. With her long gold chain wrapped once around her neck and gold hoop earrings and bracelet, she thought she looked rather chic. She decided to wear the outfit to the ranch party.

A pucker appeared between Linda's eyebrows as she contemplated her attire in the great, shield-shaped mirror. With her head feeling better, why couldn't she remember wearing these clothes before? If only the veil would lift from her mind before she left Spain. Suppose it didn't?

Suddenly the thought of returning to the United States filled her with anxiety. What was she going back to? Did she have a nice apartment with her own furniture, or did she live in a furnished room? Was her life lonely? The fact that she hadn't listed a name on her passport in the event of an emergency seemed to indicate there was no special man in her life or even a special friend.

The brown eyes looking back from her reflection widened fearfully as Linda realized returning home wasn't all that simple. She really hadn't given it much thought. *Home.* It was just a word, evoking no personal pictures in her mind, no emotions. Her room here in the *Casa* was more home to her than the home she could not remember.

Why, this *Casa* was actually the only home she knew!

Turning from the mirror, lower lip caught between her teeth, Linda wondered why she felt so mixed-up all of a sudden. She liked Andalusia and was quickly becoming accustomed to the life here, but the United

States was her homeland. Didn't she want to return there?

On her way downstairs, Linda met Doña Josefa, who eyed her coldly. Linda knew she was recalling that kiss in the courtyard. The older woman did not like it one bit that her brother was attracted to the *norte americana*.

Was it because she was a foreigner? Or because the Doña didn't wholly trust her in the matter of her amnesia? Was she afraid her precious brother might fall in love with Linda? Perhaps she was hoping he would never marry, for then she no longer would be mistress of this beautiful mansion.

Sighing, Linda headed for the library to return *Death in the Afternoon*. The door was open. She paused on the threshold. Don Diego was sitting motionless at the desk, his head bowed between his hands like one meditating a worrisome problem.

A yearning to comfort him swept over Linda. It was a disturbing reaction, for she wanted nothing so much as to be cool and composed in his presence.

He must have sensed her nearness, for as she retreated quietly backward, he looked up and saw her.

"I. . .I just wanted to return a book I borrowed."

He stood up, his glance going to the volume in her hand. "The one I recommended? What did you think of it?"

Linda went forward. "It's a terrific book," she admitted, moving toward the bookshelves. "Quite an education in itself." She replaced the volume and turned to face the Don. "I understand now what bullfighting is all about, and I'm still against it. It's brutal and dangerous. I hate to think of Juanito living the life of a *torero*. It's so filled with tension that it's a wonder all bullfighters don't have ulcers."

"Everything has its disadvantages, señorita. I will make sure Juanito knows what they are. But to those interested in the *corrida* as a career, the advantages outweigh the disadvantages. A top *matador* can get eighty to one hundred engagements in a single season, from March to October, and enjoy life the rest of the time. He is paid well and can become a rich man within a few years, not to mention the fame and adulation he receives."

"Mothers and wives must die a thousand deaths every time their loved ones enter the ring." Linda shuddered. "From what I've read, most bullfighters suffer wounds from the horns. I do hope Juanito changes his mind. He's such an intelligent boy, he could put his life to better use. Where is he now?"

"Riding his horse."

"That reminds me, may I take Dulzura when I want to ride?"

"Why not?" the Don said graciously. "She is gentle enough. But do not get lost."

"Thank you. I think I'll listen to some of your music albums. You don't mind, do you?"

"Please, enjoy them. You like classical music?"

"Very much. Andrés Segovia is—was—truly marvelous on the guitar, wasn't he?"

"*Sí*, a master. I could listen to him by the hour."

Linda left the Don feeling relieved at the way their encounter had gone. He had helped her through it with typical Spanish courtesy, though what he thought of her after her ardent response to his kiss the night before was another matter. Just thinking about it made her blush. She hurried into the *sala principal* to drown the memory in beautiful sounds.

At dinner that evening, Linda was aware that Doña Josefa's wariness toward her had increased. She caught the woman studying her with a speculative gleam in her eyes that made her shiver.

The Sunday get-together at Francisco's ranch began after *siesta*, and guests were already there when Linda and the Halcóns arrived. Mariana and her mother met them at the door with open arms. In her lavender dress with its full skirt frilled in white lace and with a pink rose in her long black hair, Mariana made a pretty picture. The young girl's eyes were sparkling in anticipation of seeing Pablo, who was on his way from Seville. He and his family were to stay the night, she whispered to Linda.

They went into the living room, where Linda was introduced to several families from nearby farms and ranches. Many admiring glances lingered on her blond hair. The men wore informal clothing, whereas the women were dressed up a bit more in short or long dresses. Some of the older folks did not speak English, and the buzz of conversation was predominantly Spanish.

A dozen children were present. As soon as they had had some refreshments, Manuel and Juanito took charge of them. Off they went to another room to play, all but an adolescent girl who evidently had been ordered to stay close to her mother.

A maid served finger snacks and sweet biscuits, with a tall pitcher of refreshing punch made from seltzer water, citrus fruits, and cinnamon. The elders were seated, while others stood about, talking. Francisco drew

Linda aside. "You are like a golden flower among all these Spaniards," he said, his look a caress. "How are you, Linda? There is color in your cheeks now."

"I'm feeling much better, Francisco. No more headaches. I've even gained a couple pounds. Don Diego is taking me into Seville tomorrow for my checkup."

"Have you recalled anything new?"

"No," she said sadly.

"The concussion must still be in the process of healing. It is only, what, two weeks since you were injured?"

"Today makes fifteen days. I've been in Spain sixteen days in all, nine of them at Don Diego's home."

"You are counting the days. Does that mean you are eager to go home?"

Linda sighed. "At first I was eager to go. But now, I'm all mixed up. I don't know what I want. To have to begin again in another place, another house I can't even remember—it's starting to scare me. And I have no one to go back to." Her voice trailed off uncertainly.

"Why not stay in Andalusia until you are yourself again?"

"My scheduled flight leaves in a week. I feel I should take it, regardless."

"I think Diego would prefer to have all things well with you before you leave his care."

"But that could take weeks. I. . .I'd rather not stay at the *Casa* too much longer."

Francisco's eyes searched her face. "Linda, are we friends?"

"You know we are. From the day we met. Why do you ask?"

"I am wondering why you cannot tell me what is disturbing you. Friends share burdens, do they not?"

Linda's eyes became misty. Had they been alone together, she would have wept out her frustrations on his shoulder. Instead, she held back the tears and kept her eyelids lowered while sipping her punch, hoping no one other than Francisco had noticed.

"Is it Doña Josefa?" he asked her gently, keeping his voice low. "She is not an outgoing person, that I know."

"She doesn't want me at the *Casa*. But it's not just that." Linda glanced toward Don Diego, who was standing with several men at the other side of the room. Their eyes met and she realized he had been watching her. She averted her gaze.

Francisco had followed her glance. "What is it, what has he done?"

Lest he think the Don had mistreated her, Linda said hastily, "It's just that he thinks I may be exaggerating my amnesia. He suspects I intend to sue for as big a fortune as I can get. We can't go into it now, how I know this, but that's the problem I have to contend with. Don Diego doesn't trust me, so neither does his sister. But they don't know that I know they're suspicious of me."

Francisco looked thoughtful. "We must talk about this again, Linda." He glanced past her. "The de Fallas have arrived, the high point of the day for my niece. They are an old aristocratic family of Seville, and my sister is hoping for a match between young Pablo and Mariana."

Pablo de Falla was a slim, good-looking young man. He had come with his parents and paternal grandmother and had brought his guitar for the entertainment that was to follow the buffet supper later in the evening. Linda noticed how his eyes lit up at the sight of Mariana.

Francisco introduced her to the newcomers with a

brief explanation of her situation. The grandmother's first name was also Linda. Tall and erect, she had iron-gray hair, keen brown eyes, and an air of authority that commanded instant respect. Her son, Don Cortez, was a courtly man in his late forties and wore a Vandyke beard. His attractive Castilian wife was full-figured and had the white skin of many of the women of her region. Her raven hair was drawn over her ears into a smooth shiny bun low on the nape of her neck, a classic style of the women of Spain. Both she and her mother-in-law were clad in the black of mourning.

When she was seated, the elderly Señora de Falla indicated for Linda to sit next to her so they could talk. The older woman kept her eyes fixed upon Linda's face as she flicked open a lacy black fan and began fanning herself.

"The head injury, is it healing well?" Her English held a pronounced accent so that Linda had to listen carefully.

"Yes, thank you."

"Francisco said you have amnesia and that you know only what is in your passport about yourself. Poor child, it must be very trying for you. You are staying with the Halcóns?"

Linda nodded.

"And does your doctor think the amnesia is temporary?"

"Yes, Dr. Perales thinks so. I'm due for a checkup tomorrow morning."

"Luis Perales? Good man. So you will be in Seville tomorrow. You must come and share the midday meal with me and my family. I will speak to Don Diego about it." It sounded almost like a command. "And you will tell me the doctor's report. Yours is an unusual case and I would like to know how things turn out."

"Thank you for the invitation, señora. Does your son and his family live with you?" The dowager inclined her head. To make polite conversation, Linda asked if she had other children.

"Three daughters. The eldest is married to a count and lives in Madrid. She has two children. My middle daughter is the mother of five. Her husband is an attorney in Toledo. My youngest girl. . . ." The old lady hesitated. Then she said, "I have not seen her in more than twenty years. She was betrothed to a mature man of fine family and considerable means but chose instead to elope with a penniless foreigner named John Jones. Such a common name. My husband, always a proud man, disowned her. I was angry with her myself, but I would not have cut her off from her family."

"How sad," Linda murmured. "Did she ever write to you?"

"Once, that I know of. My husband intercepted the letter and destroyed it unread. He could not find it in his heart to forgive her the disgrace to our name—until last year on his deathbed." The dowager paused, her lower lip quivering slightly. "I am an old woman and my time on earth may now be short. Miranda. . .my baby. I still hope to see her before I die. If only I knew where she is. I keep praying she will try again to contact me."

Linda reached out to clasp the older woman's hand, and for just an instant it clung to hers before pulling away. Straightening up in her seat, the señora quickly assumed her imperious bearing, almost as though she regretted her moments of confidence. Closing her fan with a snap, she tapped Linda on the arm with it and said briskly, "About you, my dear, tell me what you think of Andalusia."

"I like it very much."

"And our Spanish men, you find them attractive?"

Linda smiled and nodded. "And the women are lovely," she said. Doña Linda seemed pleased with her answer. "You would not be the first to have noticed that. And Don Diego—very handsome, is he not?"

Linda shifted in her chair, feeling she had already rehearsed this part with Rosita and Mariana. "You could say that," she allowed cautiously.

"I do say it. What do *you* say?"

Don't you dare blush, Linda!

"Ah, but of course you think he is handsome. One would have to be blind not to. And, naturally, he finds you attractive with that golden hair of yours. I take it you are a working girl?"

"No doubt I am, although I can't remember what kind of work I do."

The old lady studied her through half-closed lids. "It must be quite a novelty for a girl of the working class to make her home with one of Spain's oldest aristocratic families. Don Diego is very cultured. I know the Halcóns well, since I come from a distinguished family myself.

"My husband was a leading architect of Europe, God rest his soul, and his name will live on in the annals of architecture. He designed the homes of some of Europe's most distinguished people, and my son and grandson are carrying on the tradition," she concluded proudly.

The maid paused before them with her tray, and the dowager helped herself to a glass of punch and a crisp prawn. Linda reached for a prawn and nibbled on it while she glanced about the room in time to see Pablo and Mariana go out the door. They were accompanied by the lone adolescent girl.

Linda smiled to herself. The young couple were going for a stroll, with the teenager sent along as chaperone. How careful the Andalusians were of their young women!

As the sun sank in the western sky and the air grew cooler, people began drifting out to the verandah. Soon a long wooden table was set up on the *patio*. Platters of shrimp, sausages, and chicken were brought out, and bowls of roast potatoes and onions, green beans, tossed salad, deviled corn garnished with tomatoes and peppers, rolls, fresh fruit, and several pies. It looked terrific and smelled delicious. At one end of the table were pitchers of punch and lemonade. It made for a veritable feast.

They helped themselves and sat around eating while the moon rose over the ranch house. *Patio* lamps sprang to life and night-blooming jasmine sweetened the air.

Linda sat at a round table on the verandah with Francisco and the Halcóns. After enjoying the meal, the others conversed in English for her benefit, while all around them voices spoke Spanish. Linda's pleasure was diminished by the nagging disquiet she felt when others assumed she spoke and understood only English. She wished she had resolved the matter in the beginning, somehow.

Next on the agenda came *música,* an accordion played by Mariana's father and two guitars by her brother and Pablo. Linda recognized *"Granada"* and *"Malagueña,"* and the renditions received loud applause. Pablo sang a solo in a pleasant tenor, and then everyone joined in for folk singing. After that, the children entertained as a chorus with several popular songs.

By the time the party broke up, it was nearing midnight. While saying her goodbyes and appreciation for a lovely evening, Linda whispered to Francisco that she would be back soon to discuss something with him. *Perhaps,* she thought, *he could advise her concerning her situation at the Casa.*

Still, when she took the flight home she would be done with the *Casa* and its master. Dr. Perales would surely find her physically fit for the journey, and then she could tell Don Diego she was leaving. That would be his cue to offer a settlement and get her off his hands.

It was late and Linda was sleepy by the time she got into bed. "Good night, dear Lord," she whispered drowsily. "Thank You for a lovely time."

She turned off the bedside lamp. As she closed her eyes, Romans 8:28 entered her mind: "And we know that in all things God works for the good of those who love him. . . ."

She smiled. Such comforting words. Whether she returned to the States or remained in Spain, God would work out her problems for her good, amnesia and all.

nine

Don Diego and Linda arrived in Seville almost two hours before Linda's appointment with her doctor, leaving them time for some sightseeing. The Don drove to the Old World district called Santa Cruz and, after parking the station wagon, he and Linda wandered through narrow winding byways, emerging into sudden plazas where orange trees shaded splashing fountains.

They viewed dignified homes, where windows hid behind curved iron grilles bristling with spikes, and every whitewashed garden wall had its wrought-iron lantern and its overflow of vines. Through iron grillework doors, they caught glimpses of flagstone *patios* splashed with the colors of geraniums and azaleas and the water of drowsy fountains. Fine old houses mingled with secondhand stalls and antique shops. To Linda, it seemed like a setting for an operetta.

"You said the artist Murillo lived here? No wonder," she remarked to her escort. "It's a charming place. I wouldn't mind living here myself."

"Murillo was a native Andalusian, born in Seville, which may be why he painted with such warmth. After we visit the de Fallas, I will take you to the cathedral and one or two other places of interest. You might as well see what you can of Seville while we are here. I told my sister not to expect us home for dinner, so we can take our time."

"Thank you, señor. It sounds like it's going to be a

most interesting day." Linda gave him a smile of gratitude and received an entirely friendly smile in return.
He could be such good company, she thought, *when
cynicism was laid aside.* The drive to Seville had been
a pleasure.

The Don had told her interesting things about other
parts of Spain, and how Andalusia surpassed the rest of
the country in music and dance. He'd described how
the Spanish people enjoyed celebrating their religious
holidays with processions, street bands, flowers, and
song. He had even admitted wryly that Linda was a
natural blond, according to the light part in her hair.

At Dr. Perales' office, Linda and Rosita greeted each
other like old friends.

"It's good to see you, Rosita. I must say Dr. Perales'
gain is the hospital's loss. I can see you're happy in
your new job. In fact, you look radiant."

Rosita drew Linda into a small side room so they could
have a few words in private. "If I'm radiant, it's because the doctor and I are going to be married. We're
planning a formal announcement of our engagement
during the Christmas season."

"I'm glad for you, Rosita."

"Thank you. And how are things going with you,
Linda? You're looking so much better. Memories? Not
yet? Give it time. Anything cooking with Prince Charming? No? Well, I'm going to keep right on hoping. Wish
we could talk more, but I've got to get back to a patient
in the dressing room."

Linda returned to the waiting room and sat beside Don
Diego. He glanced up from the magazine he was leaf-
ing through. "One would think you and the nurse had
known each other for years."

"We became good friends at the hospital. There are

bells in the near future for her and Dr. Perales."

"A wedding? Well, good luck to them."

"I think they're right for each other. I sensed kindness in Dr. Perales from my first day in the hospital. Anyone who is kind is bound to be considerate of the other person."

"Like Francisco?"

"Yes. He's the perfect example of a considerate man."

"You and he are on a first name basis, eh? I noticed that last night."

"At my request. Americans are not as formal as Europeans." Linda paused as Rosita appeared in the doorway to call in the next patient, an elderly gentleman. That left Linda alone in the waiting room with the Don. She continued, "I like Francisco very much and consider him my friend."

"Friend?" The Don quirked an eyebrow at her. "Surely you are aware that Francisco is seriously interested in you?"

"I'm aware, of course, but he isn't pressuring me in any way. He's a perfect gentleman."

"Also a bit of a fool. I would certainly pressure a girl if I wanted to marry her and knew she would soon be leaving the country. I would make every minute count—court her and woo her until she became mine. When a man wants something, he must go after it and let nothing stand in his way."

"Francisco is not aggressive like you," Linda said, leaping to her friend's defense. "Besides, he understands how insecure and vulnerable I am at this time. I. . .I've developed conflicting emotions about returning to the United States. Remember when you asked me how I could be eager to go home since home was just a blank in my mind? Well, that's how I feel now. Going back to a blank scares me. Francisco, you see, isn't the sort to take advantage of my uncertainties. He's too kind and considerate for that."

"And I am not? Speak up," the Don demanded. "Since we do not think alike, I am curious as to how you view me."

"Since you ask, you seem to equate kindness with being soft, unmanly. I find you opinionated, biased, and somewhat arrogant—" Linda paused abruptly, aware that she had said more than intended. "I'm sorry. I'm sure you have fine qualities also."

"Let us hope so." His smile held cynical amusement.

She clasped her hands on her lap and looked down at them to avoid his eyes.

"Well, I did ask you to speak up," he said. "Can it be I was hoping for a compliment from my lovely American guest?"

She looked up at him. "Taking full responsibility for me, so much so as to bring me into your home, reveals one of your fine qualities, señor. You could have placed me in someone else's care. And you're a man of integrity. Dr. Perales told me that. I believe it. Francisco also has said nice things about you. And I know you like him in spite of his 'soft' qualities."

Don Diego nodded. "One cannot help liking him. He is all heart and also a man of integrity. Sometimes I wish I could be more like him. Just a little," he added hastily, which made Linda giggle.

You're so utterly masculine, strong in every way. I would feel safe and secure with a man like you, if only you could be more flexible. You rather overwhelm me, Diego Halcón, yet I find you fascinating.

As if in answer to her thoughts, Linda seemed to hear again Mariana's voice, "Can you be in love with this man and not know it?"

She was glad Rosita called to her just then, giving her a temporary escape from that disturbing question.

Dr. Perales gave Linda a thorough examination, asked some questions, and announced she was coming along satisfactorily.

"Yet my mind is still blank," she complained.

"We will discuss that in my office. In the presence of Don Diego, if you don't mind, since he is involved in this."

Seated behind his desk in the office, the doctor repeated for Don Diego's benefit his satisfaction regarding Linda's physical condition.

"Now about your amnesia, Miss Monroe, you mentioned a brief flash of memory concerning a favorite melody. I find that encouraging. It may be that memory will come to you a little at a time rather than all at once."

"I want so much to recall my past before I go home," Linda said wistfully. "And if I took my scheduled flight, I'd still have my job at the art gallery."

She jerked up in her chair. "Art gallery! I work at an art gallery!"

Dr. Perales nodded with a broad smile. "You see? It is coming."

She relaxed. "Hmm, what art gallery? In White Plains, New York, where I live? I. . .think so. Oh, dear, it's so vague—just a glimmer."

Linda was aware that Don Diego was staring at her intently, as if trying to see into her mind through her eyes. Was he wondering if this was part of her act?

Tell him right now that you're going home next week. Tell him in front of the doctor. That ought to put an end to his suspicions.

She opened her mouth but the words would not come.

Her resolve was melting like butter on warm toast. She did not want to be on that flight next week, did not want to leave Spain, not yet. Surely if she kept remembering bits and pieces, Don Diego would have to conclude that her condition was authentic. If she were faking amnesia for monetary reasons, she would not admit to remembering anything at all.

Anyway, she still had a week to decide. Perhaps by then she would recall more and be eager to get back home. Meanwhile, she wouldn't commit herself one way or the other.

With the reversal of her previous decision came a great feeling of relief, as though a pall had lifted from her spirit. Linda did not try to analyze her change in mood.

The de Falla villa was on the outskirts of the city, an impressive white structure containing grillework and many arches built around a series of central courtyards. The main courtyard held a pool and was paved in rose marble with walls tiled in deep blue. Oleanders, roses, and cape jessamine bloomed in enormous jars.

During luncheon, Linda reflected on how well the Spaniards savored life. They made of their meals something special to look forward to, lingering over them while enjoying family fellowship. No gulping down a hamburger and cola, no rushing to get things done the way Americans were inclined to do.

Don Diego had told Linda that in Spain it was an age-old custom not to hurry. Foreigners might think it denoted laziness, but in truth things were getting done in Spain and done well—highways, modern apartments, hotels, thermal and nuclear power stations.

While enjoying her meal, Linda had an opportunity to study the de Fallas. Don Cortez was distinguished-looking in his Vandyke beard and mustache, slightly tinged with silver. His manners were impeccable, and his voice was deep and resonant.

Linda was glad he lacked the imperious attitude of his mother. Not that she disliked the dowager; she just wasn't entirely comfortable in her presence. Pride clung like a royal robe about the older woman, making Linda conscious of the social gulf between them. She was here only because of Don Diego.

Doña Anita, the wife of Don Cortez, was gracious but reserved. In contrast, their son, Pablo, was talkative and very cordial. Linda felt at ease with him.

After hearing the results of her checkup with Dr. Perales, the elder señora expressed keen interest that Linda had had one or two glimpses into her past. It seemed to her a sign that all would be well. She then told Don Diego he ought to take care of Linda until full memory returned. He replied that he intended on doing just that, so as not to have the young lady on his conscience once she left.

Joy filled Linda's heart that Don Diego was taking the matter out of her hands, that she would not have to leave this country she was beginning to love.

Later, after leaving the de Fallas, Linda brought up the subject hesitantly to Don Diego. "You want me to remain in your home until I remember my past?"

"Why not?"

"Who can say how long that may be?" she reminded him. "My plane leaves next week, you know."

"Were you thinking of being on it?"

"I've seriously considered it."

"Oh?" She could read the skepticism in his sidelong glance. "In any case, I could not let you leave so soon. Since you seem fond of Andalusia, why not remain until you are yourself again? Consider it a long vacation with all expenses paid."

Linda stared at his profile, puzzled. He seemed sincerely concerned for her welfare, yet he was still uncertain about her honesty.

What can I do to gain his trust?

Clearing her throat, she said, "Señor Halcón, I'll stay a while longer if you think I should. But I want you to know I'm ready to leave on my flight next week if you change your mind—whether my condition remains the same or not."

The look he turned upon her was penetrating. He did not reply, but his features softened a little.

"I'll probably lose my job," she murmured.

"You will leave here well reimbursed. I have been in touch with my car insurance company. They have been checking things out and wish to make a settlement on you. Out of court, if possible. I requested they wait before contacting you until you had a chance to recuperate." He slanted a glance at her after the car turned a corner. "Might you decide to take the case to court?"

She shook her head, relieved that things were coming out in the open. "A fair settlement is all I require. I feel quite sure my mind will clear up eventually."

"And if not? It is quite probable you could collect from me personally as well as from the insurance company."

"I am neither greedy nor vindictive, señor. And the accident was not due to negligence. No, Don Diego, I have no wish to sue."

If that didn't convince him of her honesty and good intentions, nothing would. Perhaps it was foolish of her not to consider taking her case to court in the event her mental faculties remained impaired. Somehow, she couldn't do that. His good will meant more to her than money. She longed for him to believe in her integrity.

They went to Seville's great cathedral, the largest Gothic building in the world, rich in decoration and great works of art. Linda could well believe it when the Don told her Notre Dame could fit inside the building.

Outside were two features that made the cathedral unique. One was the *Patio de los Naranjos* or Court of the Orange Trees, a large, walled-in garden with cathedral cloisters at one end and long rows of orange trees that spread their fragrance through the area.

The other outstanding feature, and the pride of Seville, was the graceful Moorish tower that rose from one corner, which once belonged to a mosque that was torn down to make way for the cathedral. A splendid example of Arabic art built in the twelfth century, the Christians had crowned it 350 years later with a five-story Renaissance belfry. This was capped by a mammoth female statue representing faith, so ingeniously mounted that its great bulk turned with the slightest breeze. It was called *La Giralda,* the Weather Vane.

Don Diego took Linda up a sloping ramp to its platform, and from this splendid site they viewed a thrilling panorama of Seville: winding streets, parks, gardens, flat countryside, and the *Rio Guadalquivir.*

"How lovely!" Linda cried, enchanted. "Seville may be the metropolis of Andalusia, but it has the look of a picture book town." She pointed toward the river. "I bet that circular structure is a bullring."

"Correct. *La Maestranza.* Come, let us go now to the *Alcázar*, and then I will take you to *Sierpes* for *tapas*— snacks, that is. You will be hungry by then, and it is a long wait until dinner."

The *Alcázar,* a fourteenth-century fortress palace of the Arab kings, had been remodeled for Spain's royal family. Linda wandered with her host down winding paths edged with boxwood and beneath tunnels of roses. She viewed little Moorish pleasure houses and fish ponds shaded by magnolia trees, and a latticed summerhouse where Charles V supposedly sat and drank tea.

There were mazes with an air of mystery about them, and the palace itself, seen from a sunken garden, looked ancient and romantic with its turrets and colonnade of archways.

The interior was fabulous, carved and tiled, with columns of marble and many corridors down which the ankle bells of slave girls once tinkled. The *Alcázar* was truly a palace out of *Arabian Nights,* and like *Casa de Halcón,* shades of the past clung to it.

The Don and Linda next visited the *Calle de las Sierpes,* or Street of the Serpents. It was so narrow and winding that no vehicles were permitted. It held many cafés, where the tables stood out on the pavement and good-looking Sevillians sat drinking strong coffee and discussing business or the bullfight. Overhead, down the length of the street and fitting from one side to the other, canvases were stretched on ropes, like sails, to keep out the fierce sun.

"How unusual!" Linda's brown eyes were big and bright as she gazed upward. "I've never seen such awnings. It's so—so different."

"When the sun goes down, the canvases are furled and you walk or sit under the clear sky," said Don Diego, who seemed to be enjoying Linda's wide-eyed reaction to their quaint surroundings. "*Sierpes* is narrow enough to be called an alley, but it is actually a major pedestrian thoroughfare. Its shops are the richest in the city.

"It is a custom for *Sevillanos* to gather here socially between five and seven in the evening for coffee and conversation and for *tapas* to tide them over until dinner. Every Andalusian has learned the Arab maxim that life is much shorter than death, and so he relishes every bit of life before death takes over."

"But death isn't the end," Linda couldn't resist saying. "It's the doorway to a great new beginning, if you've been born again."

The Don raised his eyebrows. "A strange phrase— born again. Can a man re-enter his mother's womb and be born again?"

"That's what Nicodemus asked Jesus when the Lord told him he had to be born again."

"Born again. . .," Don Diego repeated the words slowly. "I trust there is a reasonable explanation?"

"Very reasonable," Linda said softly.

Sierpes was an exciting place. Something in the air communicated itself to Linda—a sense of romance and gaiety, of color and life. There were many lovely girls and attractive men with a zest for living in their sparkling eyes.

Tapas, she discovered, were snack foods both hot and cold, bland and spicy, and reasonably priced. They were eaten while standing at restaurant counters that faced the street. Linda and the Don strolled from one counter to another to taste the various specialties, stopping just long enough in each one to nibble—not gorge—on its outstanding appetizers. It was like a game, and along the way the couple met some of the Don's acquaintances, to whom he introduced her.

With her host, Linda sampled olives, shad roe from the *Guadalquivir*, chunks of cod done in batter and olive oil, shrimp, mushrooms, and other goodies.

Linda was having a good time and looked it, her face all smiles. The sudden upsweep of her glance caught a look of pleasure on the Don's face as he watched her, and she heard him murmur, *"¡Qué bonita eres!"* He did not translate, but she understood, "How pretty you are," and felt glad and guilty at the same time because of her secret.

"This has been such a marvelous day," she said, somewhat shyly.

He could not know, of course, that her pleasure was doubled because he was sharing it. Except for a few off-moments earlier in the day, he had been wonderful to her and had done his best to give her a good time.

"The more I see of Andalusia, the more I love it," she said. "Spanish life appeals to me. Why is that, do you suppose?"

"Perhaps because you do not recall your life in America. The here and now is more real to you." The Don looked into her eyes for a moment, then he added, "I wonder. . .with those eyes it may be there was Spanish blood in your ancestry."

"You called them Spanish eyes that first time we met in the hospital. Yet Spaniards aren't the only people with dark eyes. What made you say that?"

"What can I tell you? It was just a quick first impression." His smile warmed her heart; she would have liked to bask in its warmth forever.

They were at the last snack bar. Linda was still nibbling when a man tapped the Don on the shoulder and asked to speak to him privately on a matter of business. He excused himself, and the two men moved away from the bar.

Almost at once, someone slipped in beside Linda at the counter. Her heart fluttered at the sight of Sancho. "Have you been following me?" she demanded.

"Talk Spanish."

"Why are you following me!" she said in English.

"You have turned my life upside down, that's why," he replied in Spanish. "Don't you know I think of you day and night? Linda, Linda, I have not known a full night's rest since we met, and my work is suffering because of it. Whatever I do, your face is always there in front of me. I came to *Sierpes* on the chance your escort would bring you here. But, Linda, you promised to let *me* take you sightseeing!"

"That may be, but my situation has changed. Look, I ignored your letter so you'd know I didn't want to see you. Now please go. Don Diego will be back any minute."

"But you said you would sponsor me in the United States! I have always wanted to go there and earn my fortune, and you said you would help me."

"*Me* sponsor you? *I* said that? After knowing you for just one day at most? I don't believe you!"

Sancho shook his head slowly, his eyes reproachful. "So you still do not recall our love for each other? Listen, my mother is a widow, and she rents our one spare room cheap for a little pocket money for herself. We met in the garden that night after she fell asleep, Linda, and—"

"Be quiet, people will hear!" She glanced about self-consciously.

"They are too busy talking and eating to bother with us."

"Why are you lying to me, Sancho?" she appealed in

desperation.

"Lying? Are you sure of that, Linda?" His eyes searched her face. "Perhaps you will not know for a long time yet. With amnesia, one can never tell when memory will return, if at all."

"I don't think you want me to remember!" she flung at him. "The truth would spoil your little charade." She glanced over her shoulder, fearing Don Diego would see them talking together. She did not want to have to introduce Sancho.

"Go away, Sancho, *please*. And don't write or try to see me again, or. . .or I'll tell the police you've been annoying me."

"You would do that?" His face reddened with anger. "Eh, how would you like it if I told Señor Halcón about you and me?"

"You wouldn't dare!" she gasped. "It isn't true."

"You cannot prove it isn't, and I cannot prove it is. But it would set him to wondering what kind of girl he is sheltering in his home."

She stared at him wordlessly. His face softened at the distress in her eyes. "Ah, darling, we should not be threatening each other. I want so much to hold you in my arms. I am crazy about you, Linda. I think I am falling in love with you."

"He's coming! I can't talk to you now."

"You will get in touch with me?"

"I. . .I'll try, yes, but do go now!" She turned away from him, feigning interest in the last of her snacks.

"Ready?" the Don asked her.

"Ready." She faced him with a smile pasted on her lips.

"You must be tired of standing. Take my arm. We will go to the car and drive around for a while, and I will point out more landmarks."

Linda linked her hand over the arm he crooked for her and glanced about surreptitiously as they began walking. Sancho had disappeared. She drew in a deep, slow breath and relaxed. She mustn't let that incident with Sancho spoil this lovely day. As for getting in touch with him, once she left the city, it was unlikely they would meet again face to face. Resolutely, she thrust him out of her mind.

The canvases over the narrow winding street had been furled by now, and they strolled beneath the early evening sky.

"Señorita, would you care to see flamenco dancing?"

"Would I!" She sounded so like a breathless little girl, the Don laughed aloud.

"The flamenco originated in Andalusia, you know," he said. "We will have dinner where they feature gypsy dancers. They are the best."

They paused at a gift shop before leaving *Calle de las Sierpes*, where Don Diego selected a tall, jeweled, tortoise-shell comb and a black lace *mantilla* to go with it. *For a lady friend,* thought Linda, and was completely taken aback when he placed the package into her hands.

"For you, a memento of Spain."

She stared at him, speechless, before stammering her thanks, and quickly looked away as her eyes grew misty. She would treasure the gift always, a reminder of this fabulous day with the Don.

At *El Oasis*, Don Diego ordered *langosta,* the clawless local lobster, with *jamón serrano* and melon for their first course.

"I ordered lobster and mountain ham," he told Linda. "The ham is cured by burying it with wrappings in the snow of the *Sierra Nevada*. The sun cures it while the snow keeps it from spoiling. It is a famous culinary item of Andalusia. I think you will like it."

When the ham arrived, Linda saw it was a fine, dark red and sliced so thin as to be translucent. With the ice-cooled melon, it made an excellent first course.

When the entertainment started, she caught her breath at the sheer physical beauty of the gypsy couple. The girl wore a polka-dot dress of red and white, with a flounced train. She had long sultry eyes, clear olive skin, and jet-black hair worn in the classic style, with a kiss-curl in front of each ear. Her partner sported long black sideburns and wore a black suit with frills on his white shirt front.

They posed before beginning, so still they might have been on the canvas of a Goya; then the girl began to sway and click the shell-shaped castanets attached to the fingers of her upraised hands, the guitars began their accompaniment, and the dance was on.

Much like Hungarian gypsy music, the flamenco was by turns light-hearted, plaintive, and tense. The dancers performed as though they had fire in their blood. The music throbbed, and as the dancers twirled and stamped their feet, spectators followed the rhythm with their clapping hands, crying out encouragements such as *"Ole,"* meaning "Well done, that's good, give us more."

"Exciting," Linda remarked as the couple left the floor. "Are there many gypsies in Andalusia?" she asked Don Diego.

"Thousands. Ah, here comes the meal. Eat hearty."

A single guitarist had placed his chair forward in the spotlight. He was short and fat and bald, but once he began to play, Linda forgot his appearance. She almost forgot to eat, as well. He made his instrument talk and laugh and sob. His music was very Spanish, and both Linda and Don Diego joined in with *"Ole!"* to keep him playing.

"Oh, I love the guitar," Linda exclaimed.

Don Diego smiled and nodded in agreement. "I have a fine guitar of my own," he told her.

"Oh, so you play. I'd love to hear you sometime."

It was after one in the morning when they started the long trip home. Linda was tired but floating on air.

"Thank you, Don Diego, for a day I'll never forget. And for being such good company."

"My pleasure was doubled because of yours, señorita."

Exactly how *she* felt! Again tears almost surfaced, and she admonished herself for being so emotional.

They did not talk much during the drive. A rapport had blossomed between them that made conversation unnecessary, a bond that had not existed before. Linda's host was beginning to trust her, and already this had made a change in his attitude. She could enjoy the rest of her stay at his home without tension.

Then she thought of Doña Josefa, and it was as though a pin had pricked her bubble of happiness. *How would the woman react to this friendly relationship between her brother and the* norte americana? Linda wondered uneasily.

Linda surfaced to consciousness like a swimmer emerging from the sea. All was quiet and dark, and for a moment she did not know where she was. Then she realized the station wagon had arrived at *Casa de Halcón* and that she had been asleep.

Turning her head, she saw Don Diego sitting motionless behind the wheel, watching her. It reminded her of waking up in the hospital to find him sitting beside her bed, studying her face. The thought of being observed by a stranger while asleep had embarrassed her, but now it was different. They were friends.

Linda made a move to sit up, but he reached a hand to her shoulder and pressed her gently back against the seat. "Do not move. You look so relaxed, and the moonlight is on your face so that I can see you."

"When did we arrive?"

"Just a few minutes ago. You look like a little girl when you sleep."

"Have I been sleeping long?"

"About half an hour. You were smiling."

"Was I? I was dreaming about the marvelous time I had in Seville today. Thank you again. I'll remember it always."

Leaning toward her, he said softly, "Moonlight suits you. *Eres muy Linda.*"

She could see the liquid shine of his eyes. The world faded away, and she was aware only of Diego Halcón y Pizarro. Her heart skipped a beat as his hands cradled her face and his face came close. . .closer. . . .

He kissed her eyelids and cheeks, her nose and chin, and then her lips gently, sweetly. She melted against him, for he was kissing her with a tenderness that told her he cared. When they drew apart, although he did not speak, she saw softness in his expression, in his eyes, on his lips, and she knew she was having a glimpse of the side of him that he kept buried beneath his cynicism. Hope soared like a bright flare within her.

I do love him, I do! Please, God, let him love me. Let me be his rib!

ten

Several days later, Linda plunged from her pinnacle of hope into a well of despair. Unable to sleep during *siesta,* she had gone downstairs to browse among the books. As she approached the library, she heard Doña Josefa's agitated voice coming from the other side of the closed door.

Hearing her name mentioned, she froze in front of the door, knowing the woman would have nothing good to say about her.

"Your attitude toward that girl has changed since that day in Seville, Diego. Are you getting serious over her?"

"Does the thought distress you, my sister?"

"Diego! Have you forgotten that she may be a liar and a fraud?"

"I do not think she is."

"She has bewitched you! I saw you kiss her in the garden that time. Do you not see what she is doing? Why take her case to court if she can make the rich marriage? As for consenting to accept a settlement, that could be merely a clever tactic to get you to drop your guard. In marriage, she would have everything, including a distinguished husband. Don Francisco's wealth and family background cannot compare with ours, so you have become her prime target."

Her voice rose, "I beg you, put her on her scheduled flight home. We know nothing about this American girl. Why, who knows what character and morals she has, despite that innocent face of hers!"

Fury flooded Linda's soul, washing away all caution. Opening the door, she stepped into the library, her eyes blazing. The Halcóns were standing near the desk. They turned toward her, startled by the unexpected intrusion.

"I heard what you said, Doña Josefa! How dare you suggest such vile things about me!"

Utter silence reigned as the brother and sister stared at Linda. Then Doña Josefa gasped, "She understands Spanish!" Recovering from her astonishment, she said triumphantly, "Diego, *now* do you see? The girl is a fraud! She knows our language and has kept it hidden so as to eavesdrop on us. Remember that night she left the table so suddenly? She knew what we were saying about her."

Linda trembled as the Don's gaze captured hers. It hadn't penetrated her consciousness that what she had overheard was in their native tongue. Driven by anger, she had acted on impulse, which she now regretted.

"So! You understand Spanish." Diego's voice was velvet wrapped around steel. "And you speak it as well?"

"Yes, but I can explain—"

He cut her off with an abrupt gesture. "So you have known my feelings right from the start when your doctor and I discussed your case in Spanish, eh? How cleverly you have played me for a fool."

Linda's heart sank as she stared into his stony face. She wanted to throw herself into his arms and cry out that she had never meant to deceive him. If only he would let her explain.

It was no use trying to defend herself. The fragile progress made in their relationship lay shattered at her feet, and Diego wasn't about to let her pick up the pieces, for now he was certain she could not be trusted.

Women are masters in the art of subterfuge, and the ones who look like angels, they in particular bear watching. Wasn't that what he had told Dr. Perales? From his viewpoint, she had just proven she was one of that breed.

Linda felt numb as she walked away, her movements like those of a doll wound with a key.

She stretched out on her bed, and the next hour was torture as her mind replayed scenes from that day in Seville on: the sightseeing with no sarcasm to spoil it; the tender kiss and the realization that she loved Diego Halcón; the things they had shared together since—the rounds of the plantation made on horseback, the evening strolls, the discussions of her faith, the music albums they had enjoyed together, the delightful melodies he had played for her on his guitar.

He had not kissed her again, yet she had known something was blossoming in his heart toward her, even while the green-eyed monster reared up in the heart of his sister. She could sense Doña Josefa's jealousy.

The older woman's love for her brother was a possessive love tinged with selfishness. She did not want to lose him to another woman. Moreover, as long as he remained single she would be mistress of his home, in complete charge at *Casa de Halcón*. In the event the Don took a wife, a Spanish bride would expect his sister to remain sheltered in his home under his care, as was the custom with Spanish families and their relatives.

An American wife, on the other hand, might have other plans. Because of this, Linda, young and pretty, had represented a threat to Doña Josefa's security right from the start. No wonder Doña Josefa had tried to incriminate Linda as a thief.

Now Don Diego believed Linda was deceitful, for she had eavesdropped from the start without acknowledging her familiarity with the Spanish language. Reviewing the situation from the Halcón point of view made Linda blush with shame.

Heartsick, she felt the need to talk to someone. Francisco. He would understand. She washed her face, put on her riding clothes, and hurried out to the stables. The groom saddled Dulzura for her.

The afternoon shadows were lengthening when Linda came across Francisco on the grasslands of his ranch. He was sitting astride a dappled gray, talking to one of his bull hands. She waved to him and pulled on Dulzura's reins. Francisco came trotting over to her with a welcoming smile. He pushed his *cordobes* off his head, letting it hang in back by the cord. The sight of him was like balm to Linda's spirit. He was her port in the storm.

"What a pleasant surprise, *chica*."

"I need your advice, Francisco. I must decide once and for all whether to go home in a few days or remain here until my case is resolved. Don Diego was beginning to believe in the authenticity of my amnesia, and he said I should stay until my memory returned. But suddenly things have changed for the worse."

They set their horses at a walk, and she related the Spanish conversation between the Don and the doctor at the hospital, and the mounting tension ever since. She told Francisco everything, omitting only the personal details between herself and Diego.

"We were beginning to relax with each other since that lovely day in Seville, but today the Halcóns discovered I know Spanish, and now Don Diego no longer trusts me. He wouldn't even let me explain. He's so quick to turn against me!"

Linda looked Francisco full in the eyes. "He's wary of women, isn't he? It has to do with someone in his past whom he loved, doesn't it? You're the only one I can ask. What happened to turn him into such a cynic? Please tell me so I can understand him better. If you have the answer, you must tell me! Please, Francisco!"

He sighed and said reluctantly, "It is not a pretty story, Linda. But since it was a matter of public record.... It concerns Diego's mother."

"His *mother!* Not a sweetheart?"

"Had it been a sweetheart, he might have gotten over it by now. But *la madre*—he adored her, had her on a pedestal. She was very lovely, of good family, and charming. You have seen her portrait?"

"The one with the rose in her hair? Yes, lovely. You knew her?"

"Yes. Let us talk in the shade of that tree just ahead." Francisco dismounted from his horse and assisted Linda from her saddle. As the horses cropped the grass, she leaned against the tree trunk and listened to the tragic story.

"Her name, ironically, was Angela—Angel," Francisco began. "Outwardly, she was just that—sweet, gentle, and kind. Everybody loved her. But there was a dark, secret side to her nature that did not waken until she had been married some years and was the mother of three youngsters.

"It began with her children's tutor when they were small. The very first one became her lover. It was convenient with him living right there in the *Casa,* and all very discreet, aided by the señora's personal maid who played the part of watchdog. It seems several tutors came to know Angela intimately during those years her children were growing up. Had she put an end to her double life after that, the family might never have known." Another sigh escaped Francisco.

"It is said the husband is the last to know, and it proved true in this case. Six years ago, there was need once again for the services of a private tutor at the *Casa,* for Angela's grandson, Juanito. She was no longer young but still beautiful, and the tutor was a handsome rake, willing to take risks. I do not know what brought the affair to her husband's attention, but he surprised the lovers, shot them to death, turned the gun on himself, and ended his own life as well."

"Oh, no!" Linda cried out.

"The tragedy hit Diego the hardest. He still cannot talk about it."

Tears pearled down Linda's face, and the ache in her heart filled her entire body. She felt Diego's pain because she loved him. His beautiful, beloved *mamita* had betrayed his father, had soiled the proud family name, had practiced deception for years. What woman could he trust, if not his own mother?

Francisco cradled Linda against his shoulder, and she sobbed unashamedly. At last she drew away from him with a watery smile, wiping at her tears with her fingers. He produced his handkerchief and gently mopped her wet face.

"You love him." It was a statement, not a question. She saw the hurt in his eyes and realized his hopes, too, had been shattered.

"I'm sorry, Francisco," she said unsteadily. "I wish it were you. I do love you, you know."

"But you are not in love with me."

"If only. . . . You're so good, so kind and considerate."

"Everything a father should be, eh, *niña*?"

Linda bowed her head. "I. . .I didn't want to love him. It seems futile. I have reason to believe he cares for me, but he is so suspicious of me and he doesn't share our faith." Lifting her head, she held out her hands in a gesture of appeal. "Oh, Francisco, what shall I do?"

His smile was wry, yet touched with sadness. "You will stay, of course. What is needed is time for both the amnesia and the heart. If it is meant that you and Diego become man and wife—what will be will be." He stroked her cheek with the back of his hand. "I want you to be happy, Linda. And Diego also."

"You're a saint." She hugged him impulsively, and he held her close for a moment. Then he thrust her from him, gently but firmly.

"More of that and I will lose my sainthood." He spoke lightly, but the huskiness in his voice betrayed him.

Linda swallowed and changed the subject. "About Doña Josefa, I'm a little afraid of her. She doesn't like me and is trying to influence her brother against me." Linda did not explain how, nor did she mention the heirloom cross incident. "It's uncomfortable being around her."

"Understanding is half the battle, Linda. Her brother is all she has, and she is queen in his home. If another queen comes in, she becomes just a poor relation. An American wife unaccustomed to our ways could cause problems. But when it comes to influencing Don Diego, no woman tells him what to do. He will always be master of his home. As for his lack of trust in women, love will change that in time. How much time? How patient can you be? You must think on these things, Linda."

"I already have. I'm staying. Thank you for helping me understand Diego." Her eyes were shining. "I love him all the more for what he's suffered. He needs me, Francisco, whether he realizes it or not. And more than me, he needs the Lord."

"Linda," Francisco smiled wistfully, "I am willing to be second best if things do not work out the way you hope."

She reached out to touch his hand, at a loss for words, thinking he deserved to be first best. She felt humbled by his devotion that placed her happiness above his own.

At the ranch house, Mariana dragged Linda to her room almost before she had finished greeting the others.

"You are in time for tea, but first I must tell you something!" The young girl's face expressed joy. "That night of the party? Remember I told you that Pablo and his family were to stay overnight? The next day he asked Papá's permission to court me!"

"Good for him! And Papá said yes, of course."

"Of course." Mariana tossed her head and the tiny gold hoops in her ears gleamed as they caught the light from the window. "Pablo, he has *maravilloso* future ahead as an architect. He will be driving out here every weekend to be with me."

"I'm glad you're happy." Linda told of having lunch with the de Fallas and how friendly Pablo had been. "I like him a lot," she said.

"*Sí*, he has warmth of soul. I shall love him madly." Mariana clasped her hands to her breast. "He makes me feel beautiful and *muy femenil*—womanly, you know? Oh, I cannot wait for him to kiss me!"

How simple life was for Mariana, thought Linda. *You loved. You married. You made a home for your husband and reared a family. That was life. It encompassed everything: passion, pain, pleasure.*

Was it enough for an American girl of today? she wondered. *How liberated was Linda Monroe? What was her work at the art gallery? Did she study nights toward a career? If so, would she be willing to give up her plans in order to marry a Spaniard and live quietly in the country?*

She smiled to herself. For Diego, anything! *I love you so much, caro mío.* As for country life, she'd had a taste of it, and she could always occupy her spare time with an interesting hobby.

"What are you thinking? You look far away." Mariana's voice brought Linda out of her reverie.

"I was wondering about my life. I remembered something in the doctor's office that day he checked me over, that I work at an art gallery. Doing what, I don't know. Receptionist, perhaps. I was wondering whether I studied nights for a career."

"You would like that? To have career?"

"I can't answer that until my memory returns."

Mariana snapped her fingers in a gesture of disdain. "*That* is what I think of the career for married women. To make a home and raise a family—this is not a career? Hah! Is full-time job. I want to raise my own children, not leave that to someone else. Linda, do you think about marriage? After all, you are twenty-four. Oh!" Mariana brought her palms together with a loud smack. "Could it be *un novio*—a fiancé—waits for you back home?"

"No, Mariana. I'm not wearing an engagement ring.
And there was no name listed on my passport in case of
an emergency." Linda stood up. "Your mother is calling us for tea."

Stuffed olives, crackers topped with crab meat, and
marzipan cake were enough to appease the appetite until
the dinner hour arrived. Mariana's father and brother
joined the others, and talk led to good-natured banter at
the table. Then came a country joke related in Spanish
by Señor Boira. It tickled Linda's funny bone and when
she laughed heartily, the others turned quizzical faces
toward her.

It had happened again!

"I. . .I understood the joke," she admitted, flushing.

Francisco came to her aid. "Surprise! Linda told me
just today that she is familiar with our language. Her
memory is returning in bits and pieces. One of the pieces
is that she speaks Spanish. Amazing, eh? But she had
to see it in print before realizing she could also read it.
Strange, this amnesia of hers, is it not?"

Amid glad exclamations, Linda threw Francisco a look
of gratitude. How tactfully he had handled the situation
for her!

"She is going to remain at *Casa de Halcón* until she
remembers everything," he informed his family. "Tell
them, Linda, what you remembered in the doctor's
office the other day."

She did so, which got them off the language subject.
After that, the conversation went in another direction,
in Spanish, and she was able to breathe easier.

Back at the *Casa* on the way to her room, Linda paused

before the oil painting of Angela Halcón. Like the other ancestral portraits, it depicted her in the prime of life.

Angela. How lovely she was! So innocent-looking, with a soft expression in her eyes that belied the lust lurking in her heart. One could easily believe she was a model wife and mother.

And I have similar looks, though our coloring is different. Her name was Angel, and Diego thinks of me as Angel Face. I remind him of her. No doubt she went to the village church every Sunday with Josefa to keep up the appearance of piety. What hypocrisy! Her iniquity reaches out even from the grave to influence those who loved her.

"It's because of you that Diego has a negative attitude toward women!" Linda said in a fierce whisper to the portrait.

"I'm not going to give up! I'm staying right here until Diego Halcón wakes up to the fact that he loves me."

eleven

Looking back at the way her path and Diego's had crossed, Linda saw special significance in everything that had happened. Despite difficulties, everything seemed to point toward what she was hoping and praying for. Without the accident, she and Diego never would have met, and without amnesia, she would not still be here at the *Casa*. This had given her opportunities to share her faith with him and for him to learn more about her. Surely one day soon, Diego would look into his heart and admit his need for a Savior.

She must trust in God and be patient.

Diego appeared to be avoiding Linda and was courteously aloof when they chanced to meet. Conversation varied between Spanish and English when they all got together for the evening meals, the only meals Linda attended. She seldom spoke at the table, except to Juanito. He took it for granted that remembrance of the Spanish language had come to her suddenly and recently. The Halcóns did not contradict his assumption, for which Linda was thankful.

One night, long after she had retired, Linda heard the faint sound of a guitar from outside. She glanced at the luminous dial of the clock on her nightstand. It was past one o'clock. Evidently, Diego wasn't able to sleep either.

Getting out of bed, she pushed her arms into her floral robe and her feet into slippers and stepped out on her balcony. The music seemed to be coming from the courtyard out front. A chance to be alone with Diego! Her heart began thudding. Would he consider it an intrusion if she joined him?

Quickly, Linda threw on some clothes. She went out to the dimly lit corridor and down the stairs to the entrance hall. She hesitated at the front door. Slowly, she turned the handle and went out on the verandah, quietly closing the door behind her.

Now she could hear the notes of the guitar plainly, and the perfume of night-blooming jasmine was strong. She could see Diego sitting by the lighted fountain. She felt breathless at the sight of him, for they hadn't been alone together in some time.

Diego's fingers faltered on the guitar strings as he looked up and saw her coming toward him. For just an instant something flickered in his eyes—was it gladness?—but then his lips tightened and he seemed to pull a shutter over his features so that she could not read them. She sat down quickly on the bench next to his before he could rise, and said, "Please, do finish the song."

He did so without speaking, bringing the melody to its conclusion.

"*Cielito Lindo*," she murmured. "A lovely song and, yes, the sky is lovely. I couldn't sleep and when I heard you playing, I hoped you wouldn't mind if I came down to listen."

Were you thinking about me, Diego, as I was about you? Is that why you couldn't sleep? I hope so. You mustn't be indifferent to me, my love. Anything but indifferent!

Linda glanced away from Diego and up at the sky, made self-conscious by her own thoughts. A musical phrase from an old song came to her: *You and the night and the music.* . . . Could there possibly be a more romantic setting than this one?

Turning her head, she saw that Diego had been studying her profile, his expression faintly quizzical. She wondered if perhaps he was skeptical that she had joined him at this hour just to hear him play his guitar. Was he recalling his sister's warning that the American girl was out to snare him as a husband because he was rich and well-born?

"Won't you play something else?"

"The mood seems to have left me," he said shortly, placing his instrument in the velvet-lined case on the bench beside him. He closed the lid and snapped the latches.

"I'm sorry," Linda said. "It's because of me, isn't it? Do you wish me to leave?"

"Suit yourself, señorita," he said coolly.

"Couldn't we. . .talk?"

He faced her squarely and his eyes were cold as he said, "The facts speak for themselves. You have been eavesdropping on Spanish conversations from the very beginning. That does not speak well for you. Granted that what you heard me say in the hospital must have upset you. But did it upset you because you were innocent or because you were guilty? That is the question.

"If what I suspected was true, then it would naturally follow that you would conceal your linguistic ability and listen in on anything that might aid you in your play acting. On the other hand, if your amnesia was genuine and not exaggerated, you would have come clean as soon as possible about what you had overheard. It would have been too uncomfortable to continue listening in on conversations not meant for your ears."

Linda rose from the bench, heartsick. It all sounded so plausible, she could hardly blame him for having doubts about her.

He stood up also and continued with a cutting edge to his voice, "Had you not made a slip, the deception would have continued, yes?"

"It's really not the way it appears! The situation sort of snowballed and got away from me." Linda clasped her hands together nervously. "When I heard what you said to Doña Josefa about me. . .well, I was upset and so angry I choked on my food. But there were other times when I wished I had spoken up. I. . .I lacked the courage, I guess. It seemed too late for confessions. I didn't know whether it would help or make things worse."

"As good an explanation as any, I dare say."

"It's the truth!"

He studied her face. "It is difficult to know what to believe when you look at me with those innocent eyes. Come to think of it, has Francisco proposed marriage to you?"

"What does that have to do with anything?"

"Would you not do well to accept him?" he said, ignoring her question.

"I didn't, if it's any of your concern."

"Your kind of man and you turned him down? I thought you were fond of him."

"I'm fond of him, yes. But why are we discussing Francisco?" Linda's eyes widened. "Oh, I see! Your sister may be right. Is that what's going through your mind? After all, you're wealthier and a better catch than Francisco, right?" She clenched her hands at her sides.

Diego was watching her closely. He took a step toward her so he could look into the depths of her eyes, and said, "Would you care to give me a truthful answer to one very important question, señorita?"

"I have nothing to hide. But will you believe my answer?"

"If you truthfully can say you have never dwelt on the thought of becoming Señora de Halcón y Pizarro, I will believe you."

Linda's mouth fell open, and her face betrayed her by turning pink. She stared at him mutely. Unfair question! But of course he didn't know she loved him.

He made a mock bow. "*Gracias* for an eloquent, if silent reply. Since there is nothing more to be said— *buenas noches,* señorita."

He reached for his instrument case and left without another word.

Linda felt hopeless tears run down her cheeks. She yearned for Diego's love and respect, and to be his mate in a union blessed by God. A choked sob escaped her lips as she turned and quietly let herself into the house.

Up in her room, she locked the door and threw herself on the bed, whispering, "I hate you, Diego Halcón!"

And then, "Oh, why do I love him so!"

twelve

Linda woke up Saturday morning feeling depressed. After breakfast on her balcony, she opened her Bible to the bookmark at Matthew twenty-one. When she came to verse 22, she read the words of Jesus aloud: "If you believe, you will receive whatever you ask for in prayer."

A smile touched her lips and she whispered, "My prayer, Lord Jesus, is that You will soften Diego's heart toward both You and me. He needs Your love, and if my being here is only to introduce him to You, I will be satisfied. But if it's Your will, I pray that he and I will be united in marriage. I love him, and I feel sure he loves me. Please help him look into his heart and admit it to himself and to me."

In a week, a representative from the car insurance company was coming with papers for her to sign. If Diego really believed that she had planned to marry him for his money, signing a settlement might do little toward proving her integrity.

Nevertheless, she would sign it. It couldn't hurt and it just might help. Doña Josefa was correct in that she wanted to marry Diego. Hidden beneath his protective armor was another side to him, a man capable of love and tenderness, and who could be brought to a saving knowledge of Jesus Christ. Could that alone be why she was here in his home?

Linda left the balcony, swept up a handful of lingerie, laid out a lavender full-skirted dress on the bed, and scurried across the hall for a quick shower.

Her mood was still positive when she approached the library, although the sight of Diego brought on a feeling of diffidence. He wore a coral silk shirt with bloused sleeves and was working with a screwdriver just inside the doorway.

"Hello," she said shyly.

Her friendly greeting took him by surprise.

"I did not think you would be on speaking terms with me today. Will you accept my apology for last night, señorita?" He spoke gravely but with a guarded look in his eyes.

"Apology accepted."

"Thank you. One moment while I finish putting in this new light switch."

She watched as he connected wires, tightened screws, and replaced the switch plate.

"I will have to replace a fuse before I can test the lights. Have a seat." He closed the door for privacy and sat down facing her. "Now then, what is on your mind?"

"It's what is on *your* mind that concerns me, Don Diego." She made a helpless gesture. "It seems no matter what I say or do, I'm suspect. So you may not believe this, but I'll say it anyway: I'm not hunting around for a rich husband. When I marry a man, it will be because I love him, not because of his economic or social status."

Linda's eyes made their own appeal as she continued, "Since I'm going to be here for a while, can't we call a truce? You did say you wanted me to stay until my memory returns. But constant tension may be delaying my mental recovery. If you want me to regain my mental faculties as soon as possible, may we avoid conflict, please?"

The Don had kept his attention on her face during her

long speech. Now he rose and went to stand at the window, his hands thrust deep into the pockets of his forest-green trousers. Linda stared at his back, wondering if she had said too much. There was more she could say, but caution and pride forbade it.

When Don Diego turned to face her, he said, "I am torn two ways concerning you, señorita. You did practice deceit, did you not?"

"Haven't I already explained?"

He leaned against the wall and folded his arms. "Perhaps you can add something more to persuade me?"

"You are letting your cynicism stand between us, señor. Since you consider women 'masters in the art of subterfuge,' I doubt any explanation I could give would suffice for you. I can only say I regretted deeply keeping quiet about knowing your language. Later, I was afraid to confess because of your hostility toward me. What more can I say? I never intended to deceive you for the reasons your sister gave."

His eyes searched hers. "What about that other matter?"

"What other matter?"

"Your considering being my wife."

"I never said that."

"Come now, your face is turning red again. My sister was correct, was she not?"

"That I want to marry you because you're a wealthy aristocrat? Never!"

"What reason could there be other than that?" His lips curled. "Because you love me?"

Recalling that she had just that morning turned Diego over to the Lord, Linda was able to reply calmly to his sarcasm.

"Be reasonable, señor. You're attractive, intelligent,

and very good company when you want to be. Didn't we enjoy that day in the city together? Even without your wealth you have much to offer. No girl would mind marrying a man who had wealth, but to marry for wealth alone, I couldn't do that. Wealth is frosting on the love cake, but I'd rather have the cake without frosting than vice versa."

She sighed. "Y. . .You force me to say this: Yes, I have thought about marriage with you. But not because I'm an opportunist. Our situation happens to be a romantic one, and perhaps I'm a romanticist at heart, like your Spanish women."

She could feel her face heating up again, and pride compelled her to add, "It doesn't have to mean anything. Can't we be friends, señor?" Her voice was beginning to falter from the effort to restrain her true feelings.

How stiff and formal to be addressing each other as seor and señorita after that sweet, tender kiss at the end of their day in Seville!

She stood up, acutely aware of him watching her. He walked over to her, and she saw that his expression was benign.

"You have pleaded your case well, Miss Monroe. I am ninety percent persuaded that you are genuine." Smiling, he said, "You cannot expect one hundred percent capitulation from a cynic, eh, Linda?"

Linda! It was the first time he had used her given name. How sweet it sounded coming from his lips! At last he believed her. The happiness she felt was overwhelming. She wanted to laugh and cry, sing and dance, and shout for joy.

Instead she smiled and said, "I appreciate the ninety percent. Do you have time to play your guitar for me, se—Diego?"

"The guitar was next on my agenda."

It was in the library, and as he handled and tuned it, Linda could tell that the instrument meant a great deal to him.

"It's a beauty," she said, admiring its gleaming wood and curved lines.

"It is from Córdoba, from the shop of Miguel Rodriguez, master guitar maker of some of the world's finest instruments. The Rodriguezes turn out only four or five a month by hand, both classical and flamenco guitars. This is the best classical, made from Brazilian rosewood. A guitar like this one, with decorative inlay, may include some twelve thousand hand-carved pieces."

"Imagine! Dare I ask to hold it?"

He handed it to her. "You would like to play it, eh? This one is too large for you. A Rodriguez guitar is tailored for the player."

She passed a loving hand over the varnished wood of the instrument, her eyes shining. "I don't know about Spain, but in my country many women play the guitar. I'd love to take lessons. Holding it like this, I feel almost as though. . . ." The fingers of her left hand were pressing strings along the frets of the fingerboard. With her right hand she began strumming. The chord she produced was in perfect harmony.

"Ohhh!" she squealed. Moving her fingers along the frets, she sounded other chords and, suddenly, Linda Monroe was playing the guitar.

"I can play! I'm remembering," she cried, tears of joy in her eyes.

"Ahh. . . ." Diego's face was alight with interest.

She fingered an introduction to *"Cielito Lindo"* and began to sing the Spanish words in a light, sweet voice.

Diego's baritone joined in, and they finished the song together.

Linda's heart thudded as they regarded each other smilingly, for this was one more thing they had in common. The compatibility list was growing.

"One moment," Diego said, as he walked out of the library.

He returned shortly with a guitar case in hand. "Juanito's. It is more your size."

The next hour revealed that Linda could both read music and play by ear. Diego played complex melodies with his fingers, while Linda strummed chords with a pick. They then sang the Spanish and English lyrics to the old songs, *"Amapola"* and *"Bésame Mucho."* While singing the latter, Linda kept her eyelids lowered, lest the windows of her soul reveal her feelings for Diego.

How true the lyrics! She did indeed want him to hold her and kiss her and tell her he loved her and would be hers forever. She felt she could put up with anything, his moods, his cynicism, his traditions—if he loved her. She wanted to spend the rest of her life making him happy.

Diego thought she played well and offered to teach her a few techniques during the remainder of her stay. She accepted the offer eagerly, for it meant spending extra time with him.

They went out to the fields on horseback with Juanito and spent several hours outdoors until lunch time. Doña Josefa hardly spoke at the table. It was obvious she disapproved of this turn of events between her brother and Linda.

Linda could only hope the Doña wouldn't concoct another devious scheme to get rid of her.

thirteen

When the insurance agent came, Linda signed away her right to sue in the event her amnesia proved permanent. The settlement was a generous one.

The transaction did nothing to endear her to Doña Josefa, but it seemed to reënforce her new kinship with Diego. In the August days that followed, they continued to spend time together, including musical sessions in which Linda's guitar playing steadily improved.

Once or twice she caught Diego eying her as though he were still trying to figure her out. Other than that, things went along smoothly. He even remarked on her extraordinary affinity to Spain and things Spanish.

Linda had assumed tranquility of mind would hasten recollection of her past, but it appeared that total recall could take months. Still, the longer it took, the longer she could remain with the man she loved.

A few days after she had signed the legal papers, there came a knock on Linda's door as she was about to settle down for *siesta*. The knob turned and Doña Josefa walked into the room. Linda braced herself, for this private visit struck her as ominous.

The Doña spoke her mind at once. "How much longer do you intend to remain here, Miss Monroe?"

"Why. . .I really don't know."

"You can leave anytime now that the financial matter has been settled. We will mail you the check when it arrives."

"Your brother wishes me to stay until I recall my past."

"Which I doubt will happen unless you succeed in becoming his wife." The hostile black eyes chilled Linda. "I know you are out to seduce him into marriage. Ah, yes, you are a clever young woman."

The Doña's lips compressed. Her voice remained controlled as she said, "I care about my brother. When he marries, it will be for always. Marriage here is never taken lightly as in your country. When Diego Halcón y Pizarro takes a wife, it will be to someone worthy of him, a Spanish girl of good family background. And, believe me, he can choose from the cream of society. So go back where you belong, Miss Monroe. Marry your own kind."

Linda swallowed hard, trying to restrain her anger. "Don Diego is the *patrono* here. I will leave when he says so."

"Very well. It may be sooner than you think."

"And why, may I ask?"

Doña Josefa shrugged. "I would advise you to consider my words, señorita," she said. "It is best you leave . . .let us say, while Diego thinks well of you? Within the next week, shall we say?" With that, she left the room.

Linda stood rigid. Leave while Diego thought well of her? Was that a veiled threat?

That evening, dinner was served early so Juanito could build a small "campfire" for toasting marshmallows on the side *patio* adjoining the dining room.

The two women waited outside while the boy went to get the marshmallows and Diego his guitar. Linda sat down on one of the folding chairs, still a bit depressed over the scene that had taken place earlier. Doña Josefa remained standing, her back to Linda. She picked up the poker and probed the burning wood with it, staring into the flames as though deep in thought. Silence hung heavily over them.

Suddenly, the Doña swung around to face Linda, poker still in hand. "Miss Monroe," she began tensely, but never finished the sentence, for as she swung about, the swaying skirt of her long silk dress touched the fire and ignited.

Linda screamed and leaped to her feet. As Doña Josefa glanced down and saw what had happened, she dropped the poker and began to run in panic. Linda made a desperate flying tackle that brought them both off the *patio* onto the grass in a writhing heap.

Diego came running as Linda beat and ripped at the burning silk of Josefa's gown, flailing with her bare hands. The Doña had fainted, and together Linda and Diego tore off the last remnants of smoldering skirt, exposing a scorched but still intact cotton petticoat. Josefa had been more frightened than hurt.

Diego knelt beside his sister and cradled her head on his arm. They had been joined by Juanito and Pepa, who had heard Linda scream.

Diego glanced up at Linda. "How did this happen?"

Linda licked her dry lips, her heart still racing. "She was standing close to the fire. When she turned, her skirt flared out and ignited. She panicked and started to run. I had to tackle her."

"You saved her life. Your hands, how are your hands?"

"Not bad. See to her first."

He nodded and bent over his sister's pale face. "I think she is coming around. Pepa, go get some mineral water. Juanito, douse that fire and be careful."

Lowering his voice, Diego said soothingly, "It is all

right now, Josefa. Do not be frightened. You are safe, thanks to our guest."

Pepa came hurrying back, followed by a manservant bearing a tray containing a decanter and several glasses, which he placed on the picnic table. Diego told the servant to pour some water into a glass. Then the Don raised his sister's head and coaxed her to drink it. She shuddered as she became more aware of her surroundings.

Diego helped his sister to her feet and turned her over to the maid. "Take her to her room, Pepa, and get her to bed. Check her for burns. I will be up presently."

He glanced at Linda's pale face. "Come inside and let me have a look at your hands in a good light," he said.

Diego brought Linda to the kitchen's medical kit. The servants went on with their work, with occasional curious glances toward the couple.

A number of pink burns marked Linda's hands and forearms. They were severe enough to cause pain but not scarring, Diego assured her as he examined them. Gently, he dressed them with soothing ointment and bandages.

"Would you mind if I go up with you to see Doña Josefa?" she asked.

"If you like. Let me take your arm. You still look a bit shaky." As they left the kitchen, he said abruptly, "Why did you do it, Linda? You risked getting badly hurt to save someone who barely tolerates your presence in this house."

"I would do it for anyone. Besides, she's your sister." She turned her face away; how could she tell him what was in her heart, that because she loved him, she could never wish harm to someone dear to him?

Doña Josefa was sitting up in bed. Diego dismissed

the maid and leaned over to kiss his sister. "Feeling better? The color has returned to your face. Any burns?"

"Only one, and Pepa took care of it for me. It is a good thing I wear sturdy petticoats. A silk one would have ignited as quickly as the dress. As it is, I am just sore and bruised on my lower body." Her lips quirked a bit. "It seems I took quite a pummeling from the young lady who saved my life."

She looked at Linda, who was standing by the foot of the bed. "Come closer, Miss Monroe." And as Linda stepped forward, "Oh, your poor hands!"

"It's not serious, really."

"You will not be scarred?"

"They're just surface burns."

"If you had not been there. . . ." Doña Josefa shivered and reached out to touch Linda's arm. "*Gracias, señorita,*" she said softly. "I shall never forget what you did for me today."

Sitting in bed in her white, high-necked cotton night-gown with her hair loose about her shoulders and her lips quivering with emotions she could not express, Josefa appeared younger and more vulnerable than Linda could have imagined.

Why, she's just a woman like me! And still in her thirties, Linda thought. One tended to forget that. Yet behind the austere façade, the quiet manner, and plain features beat a feminine heart with hopes and dreams and longings such as other women. Was she ever lonely for a woman friend to talk to, someone in whom she could confide? Everyone needed a friend, and Josefa was isolated out here on the plantation, without husband or female companionship. There were things, after all, one did not tell a brother.

Linda realized she would never again be afraid of

Diego's sister. Perhaps, as a result of the near-tragedy, they could be friends. She was glad now that it had happened. The Doña was seeing her with new eyes, eyes devoid of hostility for the first time.

Whether they became close or not, Linda felt sure Josefa was no longer her adversary.

fourteen

When Diego changed the dressings on Linda's burns the next day, he remarked on her good fortune in escaping serious injury. Only two burns had blistered.

"I find it remarkable that you could put out fire with your bare hands and not receive serious burns. By tackling Josefa, you risked your life. Her skirt could have ignited yours." Diego looked mystified.

"I prayed for God's help," Linda said simply.

She knew God had answered, for extra strength and swiftness had surged into her hands, enabling her to subdue and wring out the flames from the silk in a way that, thinking about it later, awed her. Yes, God had been with her and Josefa last night. Convinced of it, she'd gone to sleep with a prayer of thanksgiving.

"I have a copy of the Bible," she told Diego as he worked on her burns. "I'm a born-again Christian, and I love the Lord. He's here in my heart." She laid a bandaged hand on her breast. "I know He cares for me and is guiding my life. There's a purpose to my being here in Andalusia and having amnesia. I must be patient and have faith."

"It must be comforting to have that kind of faith," said Diego. "I believe in the Trinity and that Jesus Christ died for our sins and rose again from the dead, but it is more head knowledge than anything else. I do not feel His presence as you seem to."

"Do you recall my mentioning Nicodemus that night you took me to the snack bars on *Sierpes*?" Linda asked him. At his nod, she said, "Nicodemus was a member of the Jewish ruling council, an educated man. He believed Jesus was sent from God, so he visited Him one night. Jesus told him that unless a man is born again he cannot see the kingdom of God. By 'born again,' the Lord meant reborn spiritually."

"Ah! How?"

"By repenting of sins and inviting Jesus into your life as your personal Savior. By trusting in His sacrifice on Calvary's cross, rather than your own good works, to save you from hell. Salvation is a free gift of God through His Son to whomever will receive it. Look it up in Ephesians 2, verses 8 and 9, in the New Testament. When the Lord dwells within you through His Holy Spirit, you become a new person in Christ. Heaven will be your future home for all eternity."

"A new person?" Diego was listening attentively.

Linda continued gladly. "You receive a new nature and it changes your life as Christ within lives through you. The more you read the Bible, the more you realize how much God loves you. The more you get to know Him through His Word, the more your love for Him grows. He has a plan for each of our lives, Diego. One reason I'm here is to witness to you like this. By the way, I noticed several versions of the Bible in your library."

"I have not opened them in years," Diego admitted. "What you say is most interesting. I have not heard this before."

"Should you care to read about Nicodemus, look up the Gospel of John, chapter three," she told him.

Having planted a seed, Linda prayed for God to make

it grow in Diego's heart.

The next day was a religious and civic holiday. Linda's bandages were removed and replaced with Band-Aids. She accompanied the Halcóns to Seville for the celebration. The city of seven hundred streets was never more exciting than during a fiesta. It was a joyous time of procession, prayer, and religious fervor, of home fronts hung with silks and decorated with flowers, of crowds swarming and bells clanging from the *La Giralda*. Men and women were dressed in their finest.

Street vendors were selling crisp *churros, marzipan* cakes, and iced drinks. The day was both a religious celebration and a social event, and when Doña Josefa admitted to looking forward to the holy days, Linda could understand why. Fiestas brought color and excitement into their quiet life.

Late that day, Diego and Linda had their first private moment together since their discussion about Nicodemus. They were standing in the moonlit courtyard at the *Casa*.

"Linda," he said, looking into her eyes, "I have been reading the Bible, the whole Gospel of John. It brought me closer to Jesus. Last night I went over John 3:16 again and it penetrated deep into my heart. I asked for forgiveness and for the Savior to come into my life and make Himself real to me. And, Linda, I felt cleansed after that. Thank you for telling me."

Linda's eyes grew moist. "I can't tell you how happy I am for you."

In silent accord, they entered the house.

Doña Josefa's attitude toward Linda had softened, yet she remained reserved, even slightly aloof. At first Linda was puzzled, for she had hoped they might become friends. Then she realized the woman was still anxious about what would happen if her brother married the *norte americana*.

Linda would have liked to assure Josefa that she had nothing to fear from her. But that would be presumptuous, since Diego had not proposed. Perhaps she could allay Josefa's anxiety in some roundabout way.

She went to the sewing room where the Doña spent her spare time. In her previous efforts to avoid the woman, Linda had also avoided this room. Now she paused in the open doorway and asked if she might enter. The Doña nodded from the large round table where she sat stitching sequins onto an evening purse.

"I make these for a boutique in Seville where the proceeds go to charity," she explained as Linda sat down at the table. "I also make knitted slippers, aprons, and necklaces."

"Necklaces? Perhaps I could help you with that sometime," Linda offered.

Doña Josefa flicked a glance at her without replying. They were not yet at ease with each other.

Keeping her tone casual, Linda said, "You know what I like about the Spanish people, Doña Josefa? The strong family ties. The warm sense of caring for each other. In this country one need not fear being alone in old age, not when there are relatives about. If I were a single woman with a Spanish brother, I wouldn't have to worry about tomorrow. I would know I'd always be part of the family under his roof."

Josefa's hands grew still. Slowly, she lifted her gaze to Linda's face.

"If a brother married, he would make sure his bride understood that, wouldn't he? Even a foreign bride, like

Caroline. She adjusted to living with Francisco's relatives, didn't she? When in Rome—Spain, I mean—do as the Spaniards do. Where there's a will there's a way. Right? Of course it takes cooperation on both sides and things might not always run smoothly. But nobody's perfect, after all." Linda stood up. "I'm glad for the chance to talk to you, Doña Josefa." She left the room hoping Josefa had gotten the message.

Evidently the older woman understood, for Linda saw a change in her manner after their conversation. Although still reserved, Josefa shed her aloofness and seemed more relaxed. Linda suspected she still hoped her brother would marry a Spanish girl, but at least the woman now knew what to expect should they become sisters-in-law.

September had arrived. Several mornings a week, Linda helped Josefa in the sewing room. Other mornings she went out on horseback with Diego and Juanito or she went to visit Francisco and his relatives. But would Diego ever tell her that he loved her?

Twice more she had seen love light up his eyes when they were together, although he immediately shuttered those windows of his soul. Linda wondered if her own eyes revealed her feelings for him. They loved each other, yet Diego hesitated to commit himself. Although he needed a wife and an heir, he was still struggling with negative emotions generated years ago by Angela Halcón.

Was it possible. . .? The sudden thought came unbidden, causing Linda to gasp and push it away as too distressing to contemplate. But it returned. *Was it possible Diego was considering taking a bride he did not love in order to shield himself from further pain?* Had he adored his mother so much that he was completely disillusioned about women?

Linda's hands folded in entreaty as tears slipped down her face. Diego had remarkable self-control, for the most part. Not once had he kissed her since that day of sightseeing in Seville, though she knew he wanted to. She yearned for his declaration of love, but years of prejudice and distrust would not be obliterated easily.

All that had happened so far had worked out for the good, she encouraged herself. Diego had found a personal faith, and it was obvious that his relationship with God was slowly changing his heart. She had determined to trust God. Very well, then. She would give no ground to negative thoughts. If God intended her to be Diego's rib, his rib she would be.

Several days later, as *siesta* began, Juanito brought a sealed envelope to Linda's room. A man had asked him to give it to her, saying he was a friend of hers.

The note was from Sancho. He was waiting for her in the orange grove behind the stable. It warned that if she didn't meet him there, he would come to the house to see her.

Having no choice, Linda left the *Casa* by the back way, wondering how to get rid of this annoying Romeo once and for all.

He was watching for her. She heard him call her name as he stepped out from behind an orange tree. She approached him, her eyes hostile.

"You said you would get in touch with me," he reminded her in Spanish. "You cannot just walk out of my life."

"Why not?" she challenged. "I don't know you. Can't you get that through your head?"

"Linda, Linda, you do not understand. I have always dreamed of meeting an American girl who would love me and want me with her in the United States. As soon as I saw you, I knew you were my dream girl, the one I'd been waiting for, blond and beautiful. I am not unattractive, am I? If you would just give me a chance, let me love you, let yourself love me—"

"It's time you put away childish dreams, Sancho!" Linda interrupted him. Her eyes narrowed as she studied his face. Then, with intuitive insight, she said in his language, "You would do almost anything to get to the United States, wouldn't you? I think I understand now. When you discovered I had no memory, you decided to use my amnesia to your advantage. You thought if you could attract me, I'd be willing to sponsor you in my country. You figured that if I thought we had a romantic relationship, it would give you an in with me, make me more susceptible to falling in love with you. Then if my memory returned, your lie wouldn't matter. You'd say you lied out of love."

By this time, Linda's eyes were blazing. "That was your plan, wasn't it? But you picked the wrong girl, amnesia or no amnesia."

Catching hold of her by her upper arms, Sancho pulled her to him, pleading, "I am mad for you, Linda. Marry me and take me to America with you."

"Grow up, will you!" Twisting out of his grasp, Linda darted away, furious with him for his persistence, his audacity in forcing a confrontation with her.

"Linda, wait, don't go!"

Thankful that the farm hands were not there to witness her flight, Linda sped around the stable and cut across in front of it, only to realize too late that she was directly in the path of a horse and rider.

She heard Diego's warning shout, saw his horse rear high above her, felt a flailing hoof pound against her head. . .and then the ground rose up to meet her.

"Linda, my darling, *no!*"

Although she was drifting into a long gray tunnel, Linda felt Diego cradling her in his arms. Struggling to remain conscious, she heard him cry out brokenly, "Linda, *mi vida,* open your eyes, speak to me!"

Mi vida—my life!

She could feel his cheek pressing hers and something wet falling on her face. . .and then a black cloud swallowed her.

When she opened her eyes, Linda was lying on her bed. Her head ached. She turned it on the pillow and saw two faces looking down at her, Diego and Josefa.

She tried to sit up. "Ooh, I'm dizzy. What happened?"

Diego pressed her back against the pillow. "Stay quiet, my dear. You have been unconscious. Do you recall my horse striking you?"

"Horse? No."

"First my car and now my horse," he said ruefully. "Juanito has gone to the village for Dr. Borrego. Lie still until he comes."

"Diego, what about that young man downstairs?" his sister asked.

Linda's eyes widened. "Y. . .young man?" she stammered.

Diego nodded. "The boy, Sancho Torre. He refuses to leave until the doctor comes."

Diego reached for Linda's hand as she looked at him anxiously. "Do not let it upset you. We know you rejected his advances. He was running after you, and he panicked and confessed everything after seeing the horse strike you down. He thought you were dead and cried like a baby. He is waiting in the hall for the doctor's prognosis and then he will leave."

Diego added grimly, "He is just a boy, but he could have caused your death, young fool." He squeezed her hand as Juanito ushered in the burly, middle-aged doctor.

"So this is the lovely American I have been hearing about," Dr. Borrego said, as he approached the bed. "Juanito tells me she speaks our language."

Diego made the introductions.

The doctor asked Linda if she hurt anywhere other than her head. She didn't think so, since she had fallen on grassy dirt. He checked her pulse, heartbeat, and blood pressure. Then he examined the bump on her head, cleaned it with disinfectant, and gave her something for her headache.

"How is your vision? Blurry?"

"No. I just feel a little dizzy when I try to sit up."

With an ophthalmoscope, he examined her eyes for tell-tale symptoms of abnormal pressure inside the skull, which would indicate bleeding.

"Good," he said with a smile when he was done. "I think you are going to be all right, young lady."

The Halcóns sighed with relief.

"Rest now. You will feel better the next time you wake up." The doctor put his instruments in his satchel and snapped it shut. "See that she takes it easy for the next couple days," he advised.

"I am obliged to you, Dr. Borrego," Diego said. And to Juanito, "While your aunt shows the doctor out, you go tell that young man waiting downstairs that Miss Monroe will recover and that he is to go home now. Accompany him to his vehicle and make sure he leaves."

"Yes, Uncle."

To Linda, Diego said softly, "Sleep now, my darling. We will talk later."

My darling! Smiling, Linda closed her eyes and drifted off.

When she awoke, she saw Diego slumped wearily in the chair beside the bed, as though he had been sitting there for a long time. They were alone in the room. She sat up gingerly, and he arose at once to prop pillows behind her back.

"How do you feel?"

"Better. The headache's gone, and I'm sitting up now without feeling dizzy."

"A miracle," Diego murmured. Sitting down again, he enfolded her hand within both his own. "When that hoof struck your head, I. . .I thought. . . ." His voice thickened; his grip tightened on her hand.

"You thought like Sancho? That the horse had killed me?"

He nodded, swallowing.

"I heard you call me your *vida*," she said shyly.

Turning her hand over, he bent his head and pressed a kiss into her palm. "In Spain a kiss in the palm is very significant. Linda, when I saw you fall, when you lay there so still, my heart seemed to break. I love you, *Querida*. And I believe you care for me. Say you will be my wife."

"Oh, Diego, if you only knew how much I love you! I'm your rib—aren't I, Darling? Oh, I'm so happy!" She was laughing and crying at the same time, until he sat on the edge of the bed and kissed the tears away.

"Now I know why I'm still single," she said, pressing her cheek against his heart. "And why the guys I dated never seriously interested me except as friends.

To think I came to Spain to find my relatives and found *you*—"

Her relatives! Of course!

"Diego, I remember now, I remember my past! Oh, thank you, Lord!"

She got off the bed and went to the mirror, where she stood looking at the girl with a past, a present, and a future with the man she loved. Overcome with emotion, she sank onto the vanity bench. Diego came up behind her and rested his hands lightly on her shoulders. She reached up a hand to his as their smiling glances met in the mirror. Her eyes were large and luminous as she said unsteadily:

"You don't know how glad I am that you proposed before knowing anything about me. I can never doubt that you want me for myself alone. But oh, Diego, do you know what I have just come to realize? My mother was Miranda de Falla."

"Miranda—your mother!"

"You knew her?"

"I was nine when she went away. Yes, I remember her. This is amazing!"

"To think you knew my mother! Oh, Diego, everything is falling into place for me now. And all it took was a second lump on the head. Be sure to thank your horse for me," she said with a shaky laugh, feeling both sorrow and joy as events of the past came rushing in on her.

"Come." Diego lifted her from the bench and drew her over to the chaise lounge. "Sit with me and tell me about yourself."

Held close within the warm circle of his arms, Linda related what her mother had told her and what she herself remembered.

"Miranda's parents had pledged her hand in marriage to a nobleman twice her age, and the wedding was to take place as soon as she turned eighteen. But then she met John Jones—my father-to-be—and they managed to get together secretly a few times. They fell in love."

"But your name is Monroe."

"I'm coming to that. John was a young American artist, sketching in Spain on a grant. Evidently he had enough confidence in his future to present himself to Miranda's father and request her hand in marriage. The great architect was outraged that a penniless foreigner should dare covet the daughter of a high-born family, especially since she was engaged to a Spanish *grandee*.

"He forbade the young couple ever to see each other again. They eloped, and Miranda was disowned. Her whole family was against her." Linda paused. "I wonder if I would have liked my grandfather."

"He was a stubborn old man with stiff-necked pride," said Diego. "Was Miranda happy with her American husband?"

"Very. And when I was born three years later, she named me after my grandmother de Falla and even wrote to tell her she had a new granddaughter. It seems my grandfather intercepted the letter and destroyed it unread. So my grandmother never knew about me, none of them did. My mother didn't know that, of course, and was deeply hurt that my birth wasn't acknowledged. She never wrote to her family again."

Linda paused with a sigh. "At Francisco's home the night of the party, Doña Linda told me about her long lost daughter. Neither of us knew she was talking to her granddaughter."

Linda went on to tell how her father had died a hero's death while saving an old man from a burning building. Linda wasn't much more than a baby at the time. She had little to remember her father by: a framed photograph in her apartment, showing an attractive young man with very blond hair, blue eyes, and a wide smile; snapshots of Miranda and him holding Linda on his shoulders; and some of his sketches and paintings.

He had worked as a commercial artist, with an eye toward developing his talent as a fine arts painter. The potential was there, had he lived long enough.

"I was three when my mother married Edward Monroe. He was manager of a supermarket and a very kind man. He adopted me. As it turned out, he never had a child of his own. He died two years ago of complications from pneumonia."

Linda had always known of her Spanish ancestry and that she had relatives living in Seville. Her mother had taught Linda her native tongue, including the names of the Spanish dishes she occasionally cooked. Linda took up the language in school as well and became proficient in it. She learned to sew and play the guitar, and sometimes she dreamed of visiting Spain, although it seemed unlikely.

Miranda remained bitter that her family had rejected John, whom she had loved dearly. She felt they had rejected his child as well by ignoring Linda's birth. Even Miranda's brothers and sisters had opposed her marriage, so she let the years slip by without contacting any of them.

"Then," Linda continued sadly, "when I was seventeen and she was dying of an inoperable brain tumor, she decided I should present myself in person to my relatives in Seville so they would know me and include me in the family will. She said it was my birthright. But with medical expenses and all, there was no traveling money, nor did I care to make the trip for the reason she gave. But she made me promise to go as soon as possible." Another pause, gathering more memories.

"After my stepfather died and I was alone, the desire to see my mother's family grew strong. They were the only blood relations I had. John Jones was an orphan, you see. I wanted the de Fallas to love me, and I wanted to love them, despite the way they had treated my mother. Come to think of it, my birth certificate, the proof for the de Fallas that I am Miranda's daughter, was in that handbag I lost. I"ll have to send for a copy." Linda added regretfully, "I'll never know my grandfather now. And it's sad that I have to tell my grandmother her daughter died."

Diego's arm tightened about her and his lips met hers in a tender kiss. "I see so clearly now, *cara mía*, the hand of God entwining your life with mine. You may have thought you came to Andalusia to see your relatives, but God had something else in mind, *sí?*"

Linda giggled and snuggled against him. "You needed your rib."

Diego drew her to her feet so that they faced each other. "Tell me, Linda, are you giving up a career to marry me?"

"No," she said. "I was a hostess at an art gallery. I believe I inherited my father's appreciation for fine art, but I have no talent for it myself and no head for business. Perhaps my talent is being a good wife and mother. But, Diego, will I ever see my country again?"

"Of course, my darling. I have been there several times. We will visit your White Plains and landlady and pay whatever is owed on your apartment rent. And we'll have your personal belongings, including your father's art work, shipped here. To think I am going to marry an

American girl who is half Spanish and that her mother's family are good friends of mine! For sure it is no coincidence."

Gathering Linda against his heart, he groaned and said, "I will be the one man in your life." His hands gripped her arms as he looked into her face. "The *only* man— you understand that? It must be *todo o nada*. All or nothing."

Because she understood more than he knew, Linda was able to respond with the very words Diego needed to hear. Looking steadily into his eyes, and with a heart overflowing with love, she said, "You are the only man in the world for me, Diego Halcón y Pizarro. My one and only love till death do us part."

For a long poignant moment he stood looking down into her upraised face, his misty eyes glowing.

"Welcome home, *mi vida*," he whispered.

A Letter To Our Readers

Dear Reader:

In order that we might better contribute to your reading enjoyment, we would appreciate your taking a few minutes to respond to the following questions. When completed, please return to the following:

Rebecca Germany, Editor
Heartsong Presents
P.O. Box 719
Uhrichsville, Ohio 44683

1. Did you enjoy reading *Angel Face*?
   ☐ Very much. I would like to see more books
      by this author!
   ☐ Moderately
      I would have enjoyed it more if _____

   _____

2. Are you a member of *Heartsong Presents*? Yes   No
   If no, where did you purchase this book? _____

   _____

3. What influenced your decision to purchase
   this book? (Circle those that apply.)

Cover	Back cover copy
Title	Friends
Publicity	Other _____

4. On a scale from 1 (poor) to 10 (superior), please rate the following elements.

    ___Heroine   ___Plot

    ___Hero   ___Inspirational theme

    ___Setting   ___Secondary characters

5. What settings would you like to see covered in *Heartsong Presents* books?

    _____

    _____

6. What are some inspirational themes you would like to see treated in future books?_____

    _____

    _____

7. Would you be interested in reading other *Heartsong Presents* titles?   Yes   No

8. Please circle your age range:

Under 18	18-24	25-34
35-45	46-55	Over 55

9. How many hours per week do you read? _____

Name _____

Occupation _____

Address _____

City _____ State _____ Zip _____

······ Heart♥ng ······

Any 12 *Heartsong Presents* titles for only $26.95 *

ROMANCE IS CHEAPER BY THE DOZEN!
Buy any assortment of twelve *Heartsong Presents* titles and save 25% off of the already discounted price of $2.95 each!

*plus $1.00 shipping and handling per order and sales tax where applicable.

·········· Presents ··········

Great Inspirational Romance at a Great Price!

Heartsong Presents books are inspirational romances in contemporary and historical settings, designed to give you an enjoyable, spirit-lifting reading experience. You can choose from 64 wonderfully written titles from some of today's best authors like Colleen L. Reece, Brenda Bancroft, Janelle Jamison, and many others.

When ordering quantities less than twelve, above titles are $2.95 each.